PENITENT

A riveting Scottish murder mystery with a devilish twist

PETE BRASSETT

THE
BOOK
FOLKS

Paperback published by The Book Folks

London, 2019

ISBN 978-1-0720-4189-4

www.thebookfolks.com

PENITENT is the ninth novel by Pete Brassett to feature detectives Munro and West. Details about the other books can be found at the end of this one. All of these books can be enjoyed on their own, or as a series.

Prologue

During its halcyon days as a bustling inland port on the banks of the River Urr, the village of Palnackie – with its single shop, post office, public house, and primary school – had for decades played host to hundreds of sea-going vessels laden with munitions and fertilisers until the economically-driven switch to road haulage saw the silted-up basin welcome little more than the occasional fishing boat or pleasure craft. But, for the close-knit community, the loss of Flora MacDonald was harder to swallow than the collapse of their industry.

The disappearance of the much-loved sixty-four-year-old widow of the village postmaster sparked a flurry of rumours, with some folk speculating that her wealth – accrued as a result of her late husband's persistent pilfering of the till – was the reason behind her departure and that, after a life of servitude, she had absconded with the proceeds of his nefarious activities.

However, under the guidance of Archie Galbraith – headmaster and chair of the parish council – the community unanimously agreed that without a car or any family to turn to, it would have been impossible for Flora MacDonald to have left the village unnoticed and so, fearing she may have taken a tumble after a glass or two of sweet sherry at the Glenisle Inn, they called upon the local constabulary to assist in locating her.

After much discussion about limited resources and a lack of manpower, the Dumfries and Galloway police force, bolstered by a group of one hundred and two volunteers, eventually agreed to instigate an extensive search of the surrounding area from Doach Wood in the north to Screel Hill in the south before deploying a team of less than enthusiastic divers to scour the bed of the Urr. After three days submerged in the muddy estuary, they managed to recover no more than a few flounder and a rusty bicycle.

* * *

For Craig McPherson, a twenty-two-year-old, hard-working labourer and aspiring amateur boxer, the decision to flaunt the proceeds of what he claimed to be the purse from his latest fight with an unprecedented display of generosity in the pub was at best foolish if not naïve.

At five-feet, five inches tall, with the reflexes of a sloth on temazepam, McPherson had lost fifty-seven of his fifty-eight bouts, the last of which saw a devastating right cross send him to the canvas with such ferocity that he was left with one eye staring permanently in the opposite direction to the other, a handicap which forced the residents of Palnackie to dismiss his claims of victory and surmise that the hapless bantamweight was in some way responsible for the widow's demise.

Lest he fall victim to a lynch mob intent on doling out some vigilante justice, McPherson – in an uncharacteristic display of self-preservation hitherto unseen in the ring – tucked his straggly, curly hair beneath an ivy cap, packed a bag, and telephoned his trainer before heading to the gym.

Chapter 1

Belying his carefully crafted image as a lowlife from the gutter with a soft-spot for super strength cider and a hatred of soap, DC Duncan Reid – dressed in a filthy grey hoodie and a tatty leather car coat – scratched the stubble on his chin and gazed compassionately at West who, despite her hard-boiled exterior, was a soppy sentimentalist with a bent for helping others; apart, that is, from the frail, the sick, or the elderly, due largely to the fact that the only thing she'd ever nursed in her entire life was a hangover.

Anticipating her stay on the Isle of Islay watching pods of bottlenose dolphins from the sanctuary of a secluded fisherman's cottage to be as relaxing as a double dose of morphine, West had instead experienced five restless days and nights worrying incessantly about her convalescing colleague's well-being and whether James Munro should be standing or sitting, walking or resting, eating or drinking, and perhaps most disturbingly of all, whether he'd actually wake up in the morning.

'You look frazzled,' said Duncan as she dumped her rucksack on the floor. 'Have you not slept?'

'Not much,' said a bedraggled West, yawning as she ruffled her hair, 'but you know what? Sleep I can live without, it's public transport that does me in, I hate it.'

'Did you not drive?'

'Of course we did, but we took Jimbo's comfy old Peugeot, couldn't exactly stick him in the Defender now, could I?'

'No, right enough,' said Duncan, 'a ride in that wreck of yours would've finished him off, that's for sure but you should have called, I could've picked you up from Kennacraig.'

'Thanks,' said West as she slumped in a chair, 'but I'm here now.'

'So come on, how is he? The chief?'

'Happy as Larry. You'd never guess he'd been under the knife for nine hours.'

'Nine hours? For a bypass?'

'Yup, and not only that, he managed to flat-line for exactly three minutes and forty-eight seconds.'

'You mean he was dead? Christ, that must've been terrifying for the surgeons,' said Duncan.

'Stuff the sodding surgeons, I was at my wits end.'

'I'm not surprised. So he's on the mend?'

'Put it this way,' said West, 'when I left, he was on his second Balvenie and he had a steak pie in the oven.'

'Good for him, he'll be back in no time.'

'I wouldn't count on it. Six weeks, the doctors said. Six weeks resting and nothing more strenuous than some gentle exercise.'

'You're forgetting, miss, what the doctors say and what the chief does, are two completely different things.'

'I know, that's what worries me.'

'All the same,' said Duncan, 'you should've stayed on. No need to hurry back just because we've a body to deal with.'

'Don't be daft,' said West, 'truth is, if I'd stayed any longer, I'd have probably stabbed him in the back.'

'That difficult, was it?'

'You don't know the half of it. If I'm honest, I'm just a bit crap at looking after other people.'

'No, no, miss,' said Duncan, smiling. 'You're crap at looking after yourself.'

'Thanks for that. Right, first things first – tea, biscuits, and where's Dougal?'

'Auchinleck.'

'Orkin where?'

'Auchinleck, miss. It's a wee town not far from Cumnock. He's away at the leisure centre collecting witness statements; he'll not be long. We've no milk, will you take it black?'

West glanced at her watch, raised her eyes to the ceiling and sighed with exhaustion.

'Actually,' she said, 'forget it. According to this, it's beer o'clock so fill me in quick and we'll catch up tomorrow.'

'Right you are,' said Duncan. 'Okay, the leisure centre. We've a body in the swimming pool; female, aged thirty-two, name of Nancy Wilson. She's a swimming instructor. The cleaners found her this morning when they opened up.'

'Time?'

'Five am. The pathologist...'

'McLeod? You mean he's on it already?'

'On it and done it, miss,' said Duncan, 'he'll be back in Glasgow by now. Anyway, he says she was in the water no more than six hours, probably less.'

'So what was it?' said West. 'A swimming accident? Did she drown while taking a crafty dip after hours?'

'Not according to McLeod. Her lungs were empty which means she wasn't breathing when she hit the water. There's something else, too – she was fully clothed.'

'Okay, so she slipped and fell while she was locking up? A heart attack maybe?'

'Wrong again. It's looking like she was tossed in the pool.'

'Tossed in? How d'you figure that?'

'The shower area,' said Duncan, 'it's like a scene from Psycho. We'll have the photos tomorrow.'

'Well, that's something to look forward to. So you reckon someone knocked her off then chucked her in the pool?'

'Not so much knocked her off, miss, more bludgeoned her to death with a king-size sledgehammer.'

'Ouch. So, any ideas yet?'

'We've a name,' said Duncan. 'A fella called Lea. Rupert Lea.'

'And why is he in the frame?'

'He was arrested five months ago under Section 38…'

'Breach of the peace?'

'Aye. Miss Wilson reported him for harassment. He kept showing up whenever she was working.'

'So he fancied her, is that it?'

'Maybe,' said Duncan, 'but according to the report, it was a wee bit more sinister than that; he never actually spoke to her, never actually tried to get a date. He just showed up and stared at her from the spectators' gallery, especially when she was taking a swimming class.'

'Sounds like a right creep,' said West. 'So, what happened?'

'Absolutely nothing. Because of his *good character* and the fact that he'd not had his collar felt before, the judge gave him an absolute discharge on condition he stay away from the leisure centre.'

'And did he?'

'Apparently not.'

'No. Quite. Okay, so where is he now? Downstairs waiting for a grilling?'

'I wish he was,' said Duncan, 'but no-one knows where he is. He's disappeared.'

'So you've been to his gaff?'

'I have indeed, miss, only a wee peek round the downstairs but that was enough. I'm not going back there in a hurry, I can tell you.'

'Why not?' said West, stifling another yawn. 'Is it miles away?'

'No, no, it's not far but it's a health hazard.'

'Here we go, I know I'm going to regret asking but…'

'Okay, for a start, his pad – it's an end of terrace on Boswell Drive – is crumbling like a stale piece of cake and the garden's like the Amazon. Actually, it's like the Amazon after a fly-tipping convention…'

'Some people just aren't into gardening, Duncan, that's why God gave us patios.'

'…and it's filthy inside, he's definitely not one for taking baths either. The tub and the kitchen sink haven't seen a drop of water in years…'

'Maybe he gives himself a squirt of Febreze instead.'

'…and there's left-over food everywhere and when I say food, I'm not talking takeaway cartons, I mean rotting food left on plates, half-eaten tins of corned beef and baked beans, and as for the toilet…'

'That'll do!' said West raising her hands. 'Maybe he hasn't got round to hiring a cleaner yet.'

'Well, he's taking his time, he bought the place seven years ago.'

'He owns it?'

'He does,' said Duncan, 'and here's the thing; Dougal did one of his one-minute wonder-checks. It turns out he paid cash for it. Twenty thousand quid.'

'Twenty grand?' said West. 'Sounds like a bargain.'

'Not if you've seen it, it isn't. They should've paid him twenty grand to move in.'

'So, are we looking for him?'

'Oh aye. We found a driving licence with his mug shot on it, it's not great but it's something. He'll be on the news tonight and in the paper tomorrow.'

'Okay, and this Wilson girl,' said West, 'any family?'

'Not that we know of, miss. In fact, she's turning out to be a wee bit of an enigma.'

'How d'you mean?'

'There's not much on her at all,' said Dougal, 'apart from what's on the electoral register. And I've yet to find anything which tells us where she lived or where she worked before she arrived in Auchinleck.'

'Well, keep on it, I've got to get a wiggle on. I need to ring Jimbo and make sure he's still got a pulse, then I'm going to stuff my face and have a beer. Give me a buzz if Dougal comes up with anything interesting.'

Chapter 2

As a consummate professional with thirty years' experience, an untarnished reputation, and a fondness for strong, sweet tea, Iain Fraser – a slight but muscular builder with a wife, two daughters, and a hefty mortgage to support – enjoyed the freedom of being his own boss. However, like many of Caledonia's three hundred and twenty thousand self-employed, he was not entitled to fourteen days sick leave, nor was he paid to sip sangria on a sun lounger in Lanzarote, and the only pension benefits he could look forward to were those provided by the state. So, whilst at liberty to choose between grafting for twelve hours a day or putting his feet up, he invariably chose the former.

To guarantee a degree of income during the leaner months, he had maintained for several years a small contract with a local agent tasked with carrying out minor repairs to a handful of rental properties, a commitment justly rewarded when, unbeknownst to him, they had proffered his name when asked to recommend a reputable builder who was not prone to sharp intakes of breath when providing quotes. As a consequence, he was pleasantly surprised to find himself entrusted with the renovation of a centuries-old, granite cottage, which, as a six-month project, was enough to keep the wolf from his door.

Dressed in a pair of khaki shorts and a snug-fitting T-shirt with a tool-belt dangling from his trim waist, he stepped from the gloom of the house on Glen Road, brushed the dust from his short, dark hair, and rolled a cigarette as a scowling, suited gentleman scurried across the street towards him.

'Alright pal?' Fraser said, shielding his eyes from the glare of the sun. 'Not bad for March, is it?'

'What?'

'The weather,' he said. 'I say it's not bad for March.'

'Aye. Right enough. Do you live here?'

'Who's asking?'

'I am. Archibald Alpin Galbraith. I'm the headmaster and…'

'I'm not interested,' said Fraser, smiling as he raised his hand. 'No offence but a name's plenty.'

'So?'

'So what?' Fraser asked.

'Dear God man, have you bought this house?'

'No, no. I'm just doing the place up; it's smashing inside. It has what they call *potential*.'

'Does it indeed?'

'Oh aye. I've just laid a new floor upstairs. Solid oak, reclaimed timbers, it looks great. Would you like to see?'

'Another time,' said Galbraith. 'So, if you've not bought the place then I assume you're working for the gentleman who has?'

'I am indeed. It's a fella by the name of Harrington.'

'Harrington? He's English?'

'He is, aye.'

'Dear God, not another one! We had a wall for a reason.'

'Well, he's polite and he pays cash upfront, so he's okay by me.'

'And do you happen to know how he came by it?' said Galbraith. 'I mean, there's not been a board outside.'

'Auction, I think. Apparently, the lady who lived here passed away.'

'We don't know that! We don't know if she's passed away!'

Fraser, intrigued by Galbraith's abrupt manner, drew hard on his cigarette and regarded him inquisitively.

'How so?' he said.

'This house belonged to Flora MacDonald!' said Galbraith pointing to a downstairs window. 'She was born in that room, right there!'

'So?'

'So she vanished eight years ago and nobody knows where she went.'

'You mean they've not even found a body?'

'They have not.'

'Eight years you say?'

'Correct.'

'Well, seven's the limit for being declared dead. Maybe that's what's happened. Maybe that's why it went to auction.'

'Maybe.'

'Did she not have any family?'

'We were her family.'

'Dear, dear,' said Fraser as he stubbed out his cigarette. 'That's terrible. It doesn't seem right somehow.'

'No,' said Galbraith, 'it's not right. It's not right at all. And what makes it worse is the likes of you ripping the place apart as though she'd never existed.'

'Hey now, steady on pal! I'm just the monkey here. If you've a gripe then you'd best speak with Harrington, he's the organ grinder, okay? Now, if you don't mind, I've a fireplace to open up, a chimney to line, and a new surround to put in. It'll be nice and toasty up there with a couple of logs burning in the basket.'

Dismissing Galbraith as a haughty individual whose ire was driven by grief, jealousy, or a loathing of anyone born south of Gretna Green, Fraser returned to the upstairs bedroom and unscrewed the sheet of quarter-inch plywood covering the fireplace to reveal, somewhat perplexingly, a brick wall which, much to his despair, appeared to have been built by a one-armed chancer using a butter knife as a trowel.

Unperturbed by the faint aroma of rotten eggs – a familiar smell which, based on experience, was probably emanating from a decomposing pigeon – he scraped out the crumbling mortar and, optimistically anticipating the discovery of something more valuable than the usual assortment of tobacco tins and hair grips he'd unearthed over the years, carefully removed the bricks, his heart thumping with nervous excitement.

Although the old schoolhouse in New Abbey had provided him with his most profitable find to date – a wooden box secured with a brass clasp stashed beneath the floorboards of the classroom which contained six silver coins, or 'merks', minted under the reign of King James VI – it was nothing compared to the sight before him. He sat back, wrapped his arms around his knees, and gazed in awe at what was undoubtedly his most priceless discovery to date.

'Nice ankles,' he said as he reached for his phone.

Chapter 3

As someone who'd suffered more than his fair share of bumps and bruises during the course of his illustrious career, including two attempts on his life – one at the hands of a drug-dealing pimp and the other as a victim of a hit and run, both of which had landed him in the ICU – Munro, who likened hospitals to the departure lounge for those on their way to Valhalla, was a firm believer that the road to recovery was best travelled at speed and not from the comfort of a well-sprung armchair.

Though willing to accept exercise as an essential part of the healing process, he was adamant that, despite the advice of the doctors, limiting any physical exertion to what they'd described as "gentle" for a period of six weeks was about as wise as suggesting he refrain from dining on sirloin, sugar, and whisky and substitute his staples with wholegrain rice, tofu, and a healthy portion of fresh vegetables.

Declaring he'd rather starve than poison his body with foodstuffs intended for livestock – and having spent five days staring out to sea without so much as a sniff of a dolphin – he left the car behind, took a lungful of fresh, salty air, and set off at a brisk pace along the two mile trek to the café in Port Ellen.

Armed with a newspaper, a tub of aspirin, and burning desire to take the weight off his feet, he secured the table in the corner and, wheezing like a pair of worn bellows, ordered breakfast with the words of Benjamin Franklin – "wise men don't need advice and fools won't take it" – ringing in his ears.

Undecided as to whether he was either, he squeezed a palm-sized dollop of brown sauce onto his buttered, bacon roll and devoured it with the gusto of a whale wiring into a seal, before perusing the paper, flicking impatiently through the pages of old news, bad news, and fake news until a minor article tucked away at the foot of page eight made him reach for his spectacles.

> *THE WOMAN IN THE WALL … following the discovery of a body behind a bricked-up fireplace at an address in Palnackie, Kirkcudbrightshire, police have re-opened the case of a missing person and launched a murder inquiry. The deceased is believed to be Mrs Flora MacDonald who vanished without trace approximately eight years ago. Rather than wait for a formal identification of the body, police have already begun their inquiry and are keen to speak with Mr Craig McPherson, also of Palnackie, who disappeared the night before Mrs MacDonald was reported missing. The amateur boxer is believed to be thirty years old, five feet, five inches tall, and of slim build. The public are advised not to approach him, but anyone with information regarding his current whereabouts should contact Police Scotland on 101 or telephone Crimestoppers anonymously on 0800 555 111...*

Munro, recalling the countless occasions he and his beloved Jean had stopped in the village for a fish supper at the Glenisle Inn after a strenuous day's walking along the cliff top path from Balcary Bay to Rascarrel, sat back and sipped his tea saddened not so much by the fact that such a crime could occur, but that the perpetrator would go to such lengths to deprive Mrs MacDonald of a decent burial.

Flinching at the sound of his phone, he hurriedly sought an excuse for his excursion lest an irate West berate him for hampering his recovery by hiking around the island. He heaved a sigh of relief as a different name flashed up on the screen.

* * *

With his towering frame and the bulk of a baby hippo, DCI George Elliot, known amongst the ranks as "The Bear" ever since his days as a uniformed officer, when his imposing stature and short fuse would send the local villains running for cover, was, despite his renown as an oppressive ogre, something of a patriarch who delighted in fostering his team with the compassion of a palliative care nurse.

'James!' he said. 'How the devil are you? We've been worried sick!'

'Och, dinnae fret on my account,' said Munro. 'I'm not going upstairs, not yet anyway.'

'I'm glad to hear it! And how's life on Islay?'

'Dead.'

'Dead? Come, come, you're a lucky man, James; all that peace and quiet. I'd trade places with you any day of the week.'

'There's a ferry at one, get yourself on it.'

'Don't tempt me,' said Elliot. 'Truth be known, I could do with a wee break myself.'

'I'm not surprised. All that paperwork must be exhausting.'

'It's not the paperwork, James. It's Mrs Elliot.'

'How so?'

'She's joined Weight Watchers. I'm telling you, there's only so much cauliflower cheese a man can take.'

'Count your blessings,' said Munro as he mopped the sauce from his plate, 'at least she's not forcing you to eat fruit.'

'Wrong again. Have you ever tried an avocado?'

'I have not.'

'Well, it's not pleasant,' said Elliot lowering his voice. 'It's not pleasant at all. The thing is James, I've a wee bit of a problem.'

'What's that?'

'Well, I've been needing to supplement the child-sized portions she's been serving up of an evening…'

'Go on.'

'…so I've developed a fondness for pie and beans at lunch.'

'And the problem is?'

'I've not lost any weight. Not a pound.'

Munro leaned back in his seat, rubbed his chin, and smiled.

'Metabolism,' he said. 'Aye, that's the word; metabolism.'

'I'm not with you.'

'Just tell her you've a slow metabolism. That's why you've been the size of Lamachan Hill for the last thirty years.'

'James! You're a genius! I owe you for… hold on a minute, what's that noise?'

'What noise?'

'I heard somebody speak. Are you not in your bed?'

'Of course I am,' said Munro. 'It must be the television. I cannae reach the remote.'

'Thank God for that, for a moment there… now you listen to me James, you need to rest if you're to get back on your feet. It's not good to go gallivanting about the place so soon after the operation.'

'Aye, right enough,' said Munro. 'I wouldnae want to risk another trip to the ICU, that would never do. So, what's the story?'

'Story?' said Elliot sounding surprised. 'Why does there have to be a story? I'm simply calling to check on your welfare. As a friend. A very concerned friend.'

'Are you hell,' said Munro. 'You've had a whole week to call, George, something's up. Now, out with it.'

Munro finished his tea and gestured to the waitress for the bill as he waited for Elliot to break the ensuing silence.

'Palnackie,' said Elliot. 'You're familiar with Palnackie, are you not?'

'You know damn well I am, George. It's a spit from Carsethorn. What of it?'

'I know what you're like, James. You're not one for cogitating in your pit so I thought you might like something to keep the old grey matter occupied. Something to get you thinking.'

'Go on.'

'Do you remember the case of the lady who vanished into thin air? The wife of the postmaster? It happened just before you left for London, while you were still at 'the Mount' in Dumfries?'

'I have a vague recollection,' said Munro, 'but I didnae deal with it.'

'Well guess what? They've found her.'

'Is that so? And where is she now? Acapulco perhaps?'

'Not quite,' said Elliot. 'She's up a chimney.'

'Wrong time of the year for that.'

'And there's not much left of her.'

'Dear, dear. Are they sure it's MacDonald?'

'Between you and me,' said Elliot, 'aye, they are. They had to rely on her dental records to make an ID but it's her alright.'

'Good job she wasnae wearing dentures. So why should this concern me?'

'Because you can't keep your nose out of anyone's business. Even if you weren't on the case, I'm sure you'd have heard a whisper or two.'

'No, no,' said Munro. 'Sorry, George, but that was years ago, I cannae recall a thing.'

'If you say so,' said Elliot. 'Either way, you might like to know Dumfries and Galloway are trying to trace a fella called McPherson. They've asked every division in the country to be on the lookout.'

'That means nothing to me. Who is this McPherson fellow anyway?'

'A young lad, amateur boxer. He disappeared the night before MacDonald was reported missing.'

'And they think he's involved?'

'Could be.'

'But they've no idea where he is?'

'None,' said Elliot. 'They've been to his old gym and all the pubs he used to frequent but nothing so far. I just thought if you sat down and had a wee think about it you might remember something.'

Munro placed a five-pound note on top of the bill, tucked it beneath the saucer and zipped his coat.

'Not for me, George,' he said. 'I'm past all that now. I've got more important things to worry about.'

'Like what?'

'Decorating. I've a bottle of turpentine in my pocket and I need to get home to finish the painting. I left the kitchen in a terrible mess.'

'Well, you've another week on Islay, James. I'm sure the painting can wait.'

* * *

Munro stepped from the taxi, handed the driver a generous tip and returned to the cottage frowning as if he'd been dealt a fistful of consonants in a game of Scrabble with a lexicographer.

Exasperated by 'the Mount's' obvious ineptitude during the original inquiry – in particular their failure to conduct a thorough search of the property – he removed his coat, cranked up the heating, and settled into the armchair with a cup of hot, sweet tea for a spot of window-gazing before concluding he had more chance of spotting a duck-billed platypus than a pod of playful cetaceans breaching the surf in search of salmon. He reached for his phone.

'Who's in charge of the MacDonald inquiry?' he said brusquely.

'Can I ask who's calling?'

'Munro. The name's James Munro.'

'Just a moment.'

Munro slurped his tea and winced as a tinny rendition of Vivaldi's Four Seasons almost perforated his ear drum.

'DCI Clark,' came the voice. 'Is this Munro? Detective Inspector James Munro?'

'The same.'

'It's a privilege, sir. You've quite a reputation.'

'That's what the doctor said but that was a veiled reference to the record-breaking fatberg I had blocking my arteries. Now, DCI Clark…'

'Harry, please.'

'As you wish. Let's not waste each other's time, Harry. I left "the Mount" years ago, up until recently I was stationed in Ayr. I am now retired and at present have absolutely nothing to offer your inquiry, but I do have some questions so, are you willing to talk or should I hang up now?'

'No, no,' said Clark, 'don't hang up. We've nothing new to report so far and everything we do know is in the public domain so ask away. Although, would you not prefer to pop in? We could have a wee chat over a brew?'

'I could, but as I'm currently on Islay I'll not be there until tomorrow at the earliest.'

'In that case, fire away and I'll see what I can do.'

'Much obliged,' said Munro. 'Much obliged indeed. Okay, so this MacDonald lady, the widow, did she not take over as postmistress when her husband passed away?'

'You mean Jack MacDonald? No, she did not. She continued working for a month or two and then she retired.'

'I see. And her husband, correct me if I'm wrong but was he not under investigation for misappropriation of Post Office funds?'

'He was,' said Clark, 'but from what I can gather that was all based on a rumour, a malicious rumour at that, and nothing came of it. In fact, I wouldn't be surprised if the whole sorry episode wasn't in some way responsible for the heart attack which killed him.'

'Aye, you're not wrong there,' said Munro. 'A man of his age, it was probably all too much for him. Let's move on. Dental records.'

'What of them?'

'Well, I'm assuming that if you had to rely on Mrs MacDonald's teeth to make a positive ID, then she had no next of kin?'

'None,' said Clark. 'She was the last of her clan. And it's a shame she had to pass the way she did.'

'Right enough but at least now she'll get the burial she deserves. Tell me, would you happen to know if she made a will before she died?'

'No, she died intestate. Everything was sold off. I understand there's some other fella living in her house now. Or he's moving in. Or something.'

'And naturally you've made a new round of enquiries regarding her disappearance?'

'Aye, we have indeed and everyone's been most helpful. She must have been some character for folk to remember her so well, like it was yesterday.'

'And has anyone had anything new to offer?'

'No,' said Clark. 'Nothing but sour grapes, from one individual anyway.'

'Sour grapes?'

'Aye, some fella on the parish council. He's a bee in his bonnet about the sale of her house.'

'Why?'

'I've no idea. I'm assuming it's because he had an eye on it himself.'

'Hold on,' said Munro. 'The parish council? It's not a fellow by the name of Galbraith by any chance? Is he still alive?'

'And kicking.'

'Was there not talk in the village some years back of the two of them having a... relationship? Him and MacDonald?'

'Oh, I wouldn't know about that, Mr Munro,' said Clark. 'I'd have to go through the file and check all the old witness statements.'

'Dinnae worry yourself,' said Munro, 'it's not worth the trouble. I'm probably confusing him with somebody else. Tell me about this McPherson fellow, why's he in the frame?'

'No reason other than he disappeared the night before MacDonald was reported missing. To use a well-worn phrase, we just want to eliminate him from our inquiries. We waste too much time chasing after folk who have nothing to do with anything.'

'I know the feeling. Well, if he knows you're after him, maybe he'll turn himself in. I understand he's a boxer, is that right?'

'Is. Was. Who knows what he's up to now.'

'Was he any good?'

'By all accounts he was the most successful failure the boxing world has ever seen.'

'So he's not likely to be working as a bouncer in a club or a bar?'

'Doubtful.'

'Anything else?'

'By all accounts he was a likeable fella,' said Clark. 'He'd do anything for a quid, he was fond of a drink, and tended to shoot his mouth off if he'd had one too many.'

'Did he have any violent tendencies?' said Munro. 'You know, as a boxer, did he fancy squaring up to folk?'

'Not at all. If you asked me, I'd say he used the boxing to vent his anger, he was generally a polite and well-mannered fella.'

'Okay, see here, Harry, I've kept you long enough. I'll have a wee think on this and if I remember anything, I'll give you a ring.'

'It's been a pleasure, Mr Munro, and aye, if you do come up with anything, no matter how small, I'd appreciate the call. I'd appreciate it very much indeed.'

Chapter 4

Unlike his contemporaries who converged with religious regularity on the terraces of Parkhead to taunt their rivals with a rousing rendition of "The Fields of Athenry" as their team sought to trounce the opposition, DS Dougal McCrae derived his pleasure not from watching twenty-two men chase a ball around a field but by deconstructing an algorithm, completing a crossword or trying to match the injuries of a cadaver with an unknown weapon.

Alone in the office with the blinds pulled against the glare of the morning sun, he sat glued to his screen, transfixed by the image of Nancy Wilson's sodden corpse, repulsed by the sight of her puffy, swollen face replete with blackened eyes, split lips, and missing teeth.

Declaring the offender to be an unhinged sociopath in need of anger management counselling, and convinced that any remotely sane psycho would have had the sagacity to leave the murder weapon at the scene rather than risk being caught with it about their person, Dougal organised a sweep of the surrounding shrubland and, in the absence of any injuries commensurate with anything as small or as heavy as the head of a hammer, concluded that the item in question was probably a mallet, a cricket bat, or even a meat tenderiser.

Startled by the sound of footsteps along the corridor, he jumped as the door, courtesy of a size six walking boot, flew open followed by a buoyant West looking happier than anyone had the right to be at six thirty-eight in the morning.

'You're looking pleased with yourself,' he said sardonically. 'Are you on something?'

'Very funny,' said West. 'I'm just relieved, that's all. I rang Jimbo on the way in and it went straight to voicemail which means he's still in bed.'

'It's not like him to have a lie-in, miss.'

'He needs all the rest he can get. The longer that daft sod stays on his back, the sooner he'll be up and about.'

'Aye, right enough, but something tells me he'll be round here before you know it.'

'Well, if he does show up, he'll get short shrift from me. So, what's up with you? You've got a face like thunder.'

'Oh it's this Nancy Wilson,' said Dougal. 'I've been analysing the damage this nutter inflicted on her body and for the life of me I can't come up with a weapon that matches her injuries. It's doing my head in.'

'Blimey, she really has rattled your cage, hasn't she?'

'Well, it's not right! Whatever he used isn't sharp, it has to be smooth and possibly flat, and it's not too small either. And what makes it worse is the fact that unless he tossed it in the grass when he left, then he still has it with him, which makes me think he might be planning another attack and if that's the case then…'

'Whoa! Easy big boy! What's brought this on? Where's the level-headed Dougal we all know and love?'

'Oh he's still here. Sorry, it's just that… look, call me old-fashioned but I was brought up to respect authority, to not speak unless you're spoken to.'

'So?'

'So as a constable,' said Dougal, 'I didn't think it my place to mouth off like a know-it-all.'

'But as a DS?'

'Aye, as a DS I feel I've earned the right to say what I like when I like.'

'Well, good for you,' said West, raising her thumb and forefinger as if holding a Lilliputian figure, 'you're like a teensy-weensy hermit crab coming out of your shell...'

'I'll take that as a compliment.'

'...but as the senior officer here I order you to eat this.'

'What is it?'

'Square sausage, brown sauce. There's a latte too.'

'Jeez-oh,' said Dougal. 'No offence but I don't think I can handle that after looking at this.'

West, tearing a chunk out of her breakfast roll, stepped forward, glanced at the screen, and smirked.

'I've seen worse,' she said. 'I think the grimmest find to date has to be the bagged-up body parts we found stashed beneath a bathtub in Wanstead.'

'That's plenty.'

'It was so vile it actually made me wretch but Jimbo carried on like he was checking an order from the butcher.'

'Thanking you.'

'But I have to say that because the bags were that well sealed, there wasn't actually that much of a stench. Now, where's Duncan?'

'Oh give the fella a chance,' said Dougal. 'It's not even the back of seven, he'll not be long.'

'Sometimes I think that boy would be better on the backshift. Well, I hope he's here soon, the food's going cold and McLeod's coming in.'

'Social visit?'

'Don't think so,' said West. 'He said he's got something to show us.'

'Oh aye? Show you, more like.'

'Steady.'

'Well, if it's to do with the Wilson lass then maybe he can give us a wee hint about the implement used to smash her face to smithereens.'

'Well, you can but ask,' said West as she pilfered his roll. 'Meanwhile, if you're not having this, I am.'

* * *

Carrying himself with the unflappable demeanour of a comatose koala, DC Duncan Reid had learned from experience that when it came to analysing the clueless intricacies of a case it was best to employ a philosophical approach based on rational thought rather than jumping to unsubstantiated and often irrational conclusions, a procedure which, despite his best efforts, was sadly beyond his reach.

He swaggered languidly into the office and paused by the door like a gunslinger entering a saloon.

'Alright folks?' he said as a cheeky half-cocked grin cracked his face. 'Any breakfast on the go?'

'On the desk,' said West with a smile. 'What kept you?'

'I got held up,' he said, nodding over his shoulder as he popped the lid on his coffee. 'I bumped into Desperate Dan here.'

With his shoulder-length hair and fiery copper-coloured beard, the willowy Andy McLeod – more Erik the Red than William Wallace – was, in spite of his appearance, a sombre individual who treated visitors to his mortuary with the respect of an undertaker.

'Blimey,' said West. 'The beard.'

'Aye?'

'It's gone.'

'Well, it was your idea,' said McLeod, 'and I figured, why not? Time for a change.'

'Yeah but I never realised your chin was so big, I mean... square.'

'I didn't come here to be insulted Charlie.'

'Sorry, it's just that... God, it's taken years off you.'

'It's kind of you to say so.'

'The thing is if we went on that date now, everyone will think I'm your mother.'

'Don't be daft.'

'I'm not. Look, I know it was my idea but just out of interest, how long would it take to grow back?'

'I give up,' said McLeod. 'No danger of a coffee, is there?'

'Yeah, course,' said West. 'I got you breakfast too, if you fancy it.'

'Thanks but I've not got long,' said McLeod as he pulled up a chair, 'so let's get down to business. Nancy Wilson.'

'Me first,' said Dougal, trying not to laugh as West's face turned the shade of a pickled beetroot. 'Mind if I ask a wee favour?'

'Fire away.'

'Would you mind running through her injuries again, just so we can all remind ourselves of what we're dealing with?'

'Well, I've not got my notes with me,' said McLeod, 'but as I recall she was in pieces. In simple terms she'd suffered a fractured eye socket, two broken cheekbones, a broken nose, a mandibular fracture, and two lateral incisors from the upper jaw were knocked out. Oh, and let's not forget about the subdural haematoma.'

'Which is?'

'A bleed on the brain. There were also contusions to the neck and upper arms.'

'So, she was restrained?'

'Aye, if you like,' said McLeod. 'At the very least she was held very tightly. The bruises loosely match that of a firm grip, but here's the thing: she didn't sustain the bruising at the time of the attack.'

'What do you mean?' said West.

'If the bruises were inflicted prior to, or at the time of death, I would have expected them to be anywhere from a dark pink to a blue or a purple in colour, but they're not. They're a yellowish-brown, which means she sustained them four to ten days before she died.'

'So, you're saying she'd been attacked previously?'

'Maybe not attacked but she was certainly involved in some kind of a tussle.'

'And that's your professional opinion?'

'It's my only opinion, Charlie. Fair play to the lass, she put up a struggle, that's for sure.'

'How do you know?'

'I took hair and tissues from beneath her fingernails,' said McLeod, 'they're away for analysis just now but they belong to the perp', no doubt about it.'

'Okay,' said Dougal. 'See here, Mr McLeod, the thing I'm struggling with just now is the weapon. I've ruled out anything as big or as heavy as lump hammer, would you agree with that?'

'Most definitely. That would've made mincemeat of her head. Besides, as she sustained the injuries in the shower area, I doubt there'd have been room enough to swing it. No, I'd say you're looking for something much smaller, something without an edge.'

'So it's not a knuckle-duster?' said Duncan. 'Or a wrench? A spanner maybe?'

'Unlikely,' said McLeod. 'Whatever it was has a smooth finish, blunt if you will.'

Dougal leaned back in his seat, tousled his hair and heaved a sigh.

'Thanks,' he said, 'but I'm still none the wiser.'

'Maybe you're looking at it from the wrong angle.'

'How so?'

'Maybe there was no weapon. Think of the walls, the tiled walls in the shower area.'

'Jeez-oh!' said Dougal. 'He smashed her head against the wall!'

'It's just a thought.'

'You lot carry on, I've some photos to look at.'

West drained her coffee, glanced sheepishly at McLeod and smiled.

'Sorry,' she said. 'I didn't mean to be rude.'

'Forgotten,' said McLeod. 'Now, can we press on?'

'Yeah, two ticks. I just need to get up to speed on a couple of things first. Dougal, have you spoken to the staff at the leisure centre?'

'Aye, miss. All done.'

'And?'

'Well, they're shocked, understandably.'

'Yeah, yeah, apart from that.'

'No-one knows anything,' said Dougal. 'Those who were on that day say Miss Wilson was her usual cheery self. They left before her because it was her turn to lock up.'

'And what about the cleaners who found her?' said West. 'Have you grilled them too?'

'Well, I tried to. I'm not being rude but English is not their first language. It was two Bulgarian ladies.'

'Just a lot of screeching and wailing then?'

'Pretty much, aye.'

'And is there anyone else on your list?' said West. 'Part-timers? Casual labour maybe?'

'No, no,' said Dougal. 'That's it. I've spoken to all the regular staff, there's only two qualified to take lessons, both swimming. All the other classes are run by folk not directly employed by the centre so they only show up for an hour or so, mainly on the weekends.'

'Okay. Good. And you say she was single?'

'Aye, apparently so. Although according to the receptionist the latest gossip was that she had started seeing someone, just recently mind.'

'And do we know who?'

'Aye, a fella by the name of Jake Nevin. He's one of the service contractors, he gives the football pitch a wee trim every couple of weeks.'

'We should have a word anyway; get him in, would you?'

'No bother,' said Dougal. 'Leave it to me.'

'Good. Now Duncan. CCTV. I assume you've checked it?'

'I would've done, miss, if there was anything worth checking.'

'Come again?'

'It was turned off.'

'You are kidding, right?'

'I wish I was,' said Duncan. 'It was disabled at 9:46 pm. That's about fifteen minutes after they'd shut up shop for the night.'

'Well, that's all we need,' said West. 'Hold up, the cameras would've caught the perp' going in though, surely?'

'That's assuming he turned up while they were open.'

'You don't think he did?'

'I'm not sure,' said Duncan. 'You see, the centre's only open from 5:30 am to 9:30 pm during the week and nobody entered the building between 7:30 pm and 8:15, which is when the last person went in. A female. Sixty-odd. Not exactly suspect material.'

'Then how the hell did the perp' get in?'

'Fire doors maybe? Emergency exits?'

'Oh use your head!' said West impatiently. 'Fire doors open outwards! There are no handles on the outside!'

'Windows then? Skylights?'

'Good God, we're not looking for Spiderman! You're sure there's no other way in? No back entrance? No loading bay or delivery area? Anything like that?'

'Nothing,' said Duncan, peeved at West's sudden change of mood. 'Which means he must have been wearing the cloak of invisibility. Like some kind of magician.'

West glowered across the room, thrust her hands into her pockets, and ambled towards the window before slowly turning with the maniacal grin of a ventriloquist's dummy plastered across her face.

'You know what?' she said as she raised the blinds. 'You're not far off the mark.'

'I'm not with you.'

'It's obvious, isn't it? Like some stunt the Magic Circle would pull. The perp', he was there all the time.'

'You mean hiding?'

'Or working,' said West. 'Run a check on all the blokes who work at the centre and see if any of them have got form.'

'Miss.'

'Next, you're going to love this, get back on the CCTV. I want you to go through the footage from the moment they opened up and clock every single person going in, then make sure they come out again. If someone doesn't show, then there's a good chance he's our man.'

'Roger that, miss,' said Duncan. 'Might take a wee while.'

'Then you'd better get cracking. Now, the only question left is that perennial favourite: why?'

'I reckon he was after something,' said Dougal, peering round his screen. 'Take a wee look at the photos of the office, it's completely trashed, turned upside down and inside out.'

'Like they had a scuffle?' said West. 'Like she rumbled some chancer looking for the safe or something?'

'No. I'm not convinced about that. I think it was more personal.'

'What makes you say that?'

'Her handbag and her purse, they're bagged up on the side there. The lining's been slashed on both of them. I'd say he was after something she had in her possession.'

'Maybe it was this,' said McLeod as he pushed a sealed plastic bag across the table. 'She was wearing it around her neck, beneath her top.'

West reached for the bag, squinting as she scrutinised the small, heart-shaped locket.

'It's gorgeous,' she said. 'Do you think it's valuable?'

'Well, it's not going to buy you a house,' said McLeod, 'but it's valuable enough, aye. It's an antique. I took the liberty of referencing the hallmark on the back, the thistle means it's sterling silver, top quality, and the tree with the wee fish means it was made in Glasgow. Unfortunately the maker's mark has worn away.'

'I don't get it,' said West. 'I mean it's nice enough but surely he wouldn't have gone ballistic over a little locket, would he?'

'Maybe it's not the locket he was after, but what's inside.'

West frowned at McLeod, snapped on a pair of gloves, and slowly opened the trinket.

'Don't tell me,' she said, 'it's a lock of… oh. It's empty.'

'It's not empty. It's engraved. Four digits. Eight, eight, one, eight. Followed by two letters: XX.'

Duncan leaned back in his chair and scratched the stubble on his chin, hesitating before he spoke.

'Four digits,' he said. 'It could be a birthday or an anniversary. The eighth of the eighth, twenty-eighteen.'

'Why have it engraved?' said West.

'Maybe it was gift.'

'There is another possibility,' said Dougal. 'It could be a PIN number.'

West looked to the ceiling and rolled her eyes.

'Give me strength,' she said. 'Come on boys, you can do better than that! A PIN number for God's sake? Why? Don't tell me she had Alzheimer's.'

'Well, do you not think we should check it against the cards in her purse anyway?'

'No I do not!'

'Hang fire, miss,' said Duncan, 'no offence but do you not think you're being a wee bit hasty? I mean, what if it's a PIN number for somebody else's account?'

'And the letters? XX?'

'They could be the initials of the account holder.'

'Genius!' said West. 'I'd never have thought of that.'

'I do my best.'

'So, all we have to do is find somebody called Xavier Xerox and we're home dry.'

'Okay,' said Duncan despondently, 'well, maybe they're not initials after all. Maybe they're kisses.'

'This is getting us nowhere,' said West reaching for her coat. 'Have either of you two been round to her gaff for a quick shufty yet?'

'Not yet, that's on today's agenda.'

'Well, we'd better get a wiggle on. Dougal, you come with me. Duncan, CCTV. Andy, how long before you get some serious stubble on that chin of yours?'

'I'd give it a week.'

'Good, we'll talk then.'

Chapter 5

As a neurotic individual battling to shed his bookish image as one of Ayrshire's closet intellectuals, DS Dougal McCrae – despite his best efforts – struggled to conceal his horror when confronted by any of his unfounded fears; the worst of which was travelling at speed in the passenger seat of a dilapidated Defender with DI West at the wheel, who drove not with the precision of a trained pursuit driver but with the recklessness of the pursued.

With his feet braced against the front of the footwell and one hand gripping the handle on the door, he winced as the hedgerow flashed by in a blur while West, oblivious to his malaise, hurtled along a deserted A70 towards Auchinleck with the needle nudging ninety.

'I could've followed on my scooter,' he said, shouting above the roar of the wind.

'Don't be daft,' said West, 'twice as much petrol plus I'd have to wait three days for you to catch up. Why don't you get yourself a nice little motor instead? You'd be all warm and toasty too.'

'No, no. I'm happy on two wheels, thank you.'

'Of course you are. Wouldn't want to tarnish that smooth Italian image of yours now, would we?'

'Meaning?'

'Sorry,' said West. 'I'm being facetious.'

'Apology accepted,' said Dougal. 'Besides, all cars look the same. Even if I did want one, I couldn't afford it. You can't get a classy set of wheels unless you're minted.'

'Rubbish! Of course you can!'

'Like what?'

'Well, I don't know. Like a… like a Figaro maybe.'

'Oh I see where this is going now.'

'I don't know what you mean.'

'What I mean,' said Dougal, 'is now that you've got yourself this Defender you want to offload your Figaro.'

'I do not!' said West, laughing nervously. 'But now that you mention it, it's not such a bad idea. Let's face it, it'd suit you down to the ground.'

'I beg to differ.'

'What's not to like? It's nippy, cheap to run, and you have to admit it's pretty stylish too.'

'Oh aye, and I'd end up looking like Columbo on his way to a wedding. Besides, I'd probably get set upon if anyone saw me driving a thing like that.'

'Well, have a think,' said West. 'It's going for a song.'

'Is it indeed? *Money for Nothing*, no doubt.'

West, one eye on the sat nav, smiled and slowed to a sedate thirty as they approached the outskirts of Auchinleck.

'So, what's the SP on this Rupert Lea bloke?' she said. 'Have we found him yet?'

'No. Not a dickie bird,' said Dougal. 'Uniform are still checking his house every day but he's still not turned up. It would help a lot if we actually knew what he looked like these days.'

'You don't reckon he's done a flit?'

'To be fair, I doubt he even knows we're looking for him. No, I reckon the fella's taken himself off for a few days.'

'It's still a bit of a coincidence though, isn't it?' said West. 'Nancy Wilson's found bobbing about in the pool and our suspect disappears off the face of the earth.'

'Maybe,' said Dougal, 'but either way he's not exactly public enemy number one, so, apart from circulating a description that's years old, there's not much else we can do just now. I mean, it's not as if The Bear is going to approve a county-wide search for the fella now, is it?'

'He might have to,' said West, 'because if he hasn't shown his face by tomorrow night, that's exactly what I'm going to ask for.'

* * *

Lined with faceless, pebble-dashed terraces sporting unkempt gardens the size of a handkerchief, Cameron Drive – a quiet residential street on the edge of the village – was a fine example of post-war planning by in-house architects designed to depress its inhabitants and maintain an air of austerity for as long as possible.

West cruised past Nancy Wilson's house and parked a few yards further up the street.

'Right,' she said, 'first question: where's uniform? Why isn't this place cordoned off?'

'Well, it's not a crime scene, miss. Besides, uniform did come by a few hours after the body was found. They said the house was secure, job done.'

'Fair enough. And where are we in relation to the leisure centre?'

'Behind us,' said Dougal. 'It's not even a ten-minute walk, back the way we came.'

'Okay, so chances are she wouldn't drive to work?'

'Not unless she needed a mobility scooter.'

West leaned back and adjusted the rear-view mirror until she got a clear view of Wilson's home.

'Do we know what she drives?'

'Aye, a green Micra,' said Dougal. 'If I'm not mistaken, that's hers parked out front.'

West pulled her phone from her hip, spun in her seat, and flicked on the camera.

'Remind me,' she said as she zoomed in on the house, 'the leisure centre opens at five-thirty, right?'

'Correct.'

'So, what time would Nancy start work?'

'Between midday and one o'clock,' said Dougal. 'What exactly are you doing?'

'I'm channelling my inner Jimbo.'

'Let's have it. Explain yourself.'

'Okay,' said West. 'If she left for work around lunchtime, then why would she pull the curtains when it's still broad daylight outside?'

'Well, it's not normal behaviour, I'll give you that. Maybe it's because she knew that by the time she got home it would be dark.'

'As it would for most people. Nah, I don't buy it. Let's take a look.'

'Okay,' said Dougal. 'I'll just give this Jake Nevin fella a call, I'll be with you in a minute.'

Ignoring the curious curtain-twitcher in the neighbouring property, West paused by the gate, pulled on a pair of latex gloves and, cupping her hands against the window, took a peek inside the Micra before wandering up the path where, in her own inimitable style, she proceeded to ring the bell and hammer the door with the side of her fist in an effort to elicit a response.

Satisfied that either the house was empty or that the occupants had slipped into an irreversible coma, she ambled along the side alley to the rear of the house with an excitable Dougal snapping at her heels.

'Nevin's on a job, miss,' he said. 'The rugby club. He says he'll be there all day but he's willing to drop by the office tomorrow.'

'That's nice of him,' said West as she inspected the back door, 'but that's no good to us, we can't afford to hang around. Tell you what, as soon as we're done here, we'll pay him a visit and see what he's got to say for himself.'

'Right you are, miss,' said Dougal. 'Here, Wilson's house keys.'

'No need,' said West. 'Look, the door's been jimmied.'

As a lover of wildlife and a keen conservationist, Dougal was well aware of the physiological responses exhibited by members of the animal kingdom when faced with a confrontational situation, commonly known as "fight or flight". As a subscriber to the latter, he zipped his jacket and instinctively took a step backwards.

'Jeez-oh!' he said. 'That must've happened after uniform left. Should we not call for back-up? I mean, they could still be in there!'

'Nah, we'll be fine.'

'Are you sure? I could ring Duncan instead, he's always handy to have in a brawl.'

'Don't you worry,' said West as she eased the door open with her foot. 'I'll look after you.'

Unlike her own kitchen which Munro had once likened to a Tracey Emin installation at the Tate gallery, Nancy Wilson's, with its cracked, brown quarry tiles, magnolia cupboards, and free-standing cooker was, though dated, impeccably clean.

'Not my cup of tea,' she said, 'but I've got to hand it to her, she's handy with a mop and bucket.'

'Everything seems to be in order,' said Dougal. 'Will we go now?'

Worried that the housebreaker was not the calculating psychopath responsible for Wilson's demise but rather a drug-fuelled nutter ready to pop out of the woodwork at any given moment, Dougal, fists clenched by his side, took a deep breath and followed West warily down the hall to the lounge.

'Blimey,' she said gazing at the upturned sofa, the broken table lamps, the ravaged bookcase, and the empty sideboard. 'She's obviously not had time to give this room the once over.'

'No,' said Dougal, 'but somebody else has, and my money's on the same fella who trashed her office.'

'Well, it certainly explains why the curtains are closed,' said West as she tip-toed her way through the array of DVDs, magazines, framed photos, and personal ephemera littering the floor.

'What are you thinking?' said Dougal.

'I'm thinking,' said West pensively, 'that this wasn't the work of your average burglar who'd try to cover his tracks. And it's not the work of an opportunist because he'd have started with the kitchen. Whoever did this wasn't bothered about leaving a trail of destruction, they were in a hurry, and I'd say they were looking for something specific.'

'Well,' said Dougal, 'that matches our assessment of the leisure centre.'

Standing with her hands on her hips, West, nonplussed, turned full circle surveying the damage before returning to the hall to examine the front door.

'This is locked,' she said twisting the night latch, 'which means he left by the tradesmen's. Let's see if he's rearranged the bedrooms too.'

'I could wait here if you like,' said Dougal. 'You know, just in case someone comes in.'

'Good idea,' said West as she made her way upstairs. 'If you see anyone armed with a crowbar, just give me a shout.'

'Wait for me,' said Dougal. 'I'm right behind you.'

Following West's animated hand signals, Dougal reluctantly glanced around the sparsely furnished spare room before cautiously nudging open the bathroom door to find, much to his relief, nothing but a bale of freshly laundered towels and the overwhelming stench of Mr Muscle.

'All clear,' he said as he joined West in the main bedroom. 'Good grief, what happened here?'

'Well, it's not the aftermath of a lovers' tiff, is it?'

'No, no. This is divorce, right enough.'

'What I can't figure out is what the bleeding hell he's looking for.'

'Would it not be the locket?'

West perched on the edge of the bed, thought for a moment and shook her head.

'No,' she said bluntly. 'Don't get me wrong, any other day of the week and I'd agree with you, but no. It's not the locket. It's something bigger.'

'How so?'

'Okay look, if a woman has a piece of valuable jewellery, sentimental or otherwise, and she's not wearing it, then she's going to keep it somewhere safe along with her other treasured possessions.'

'Aye, I get that,' said Dougal. 'So she'd hide it in the bedroom or the lounge, in her sock drawer or a cupboard with mementos or birthday cards maybe, which is exactly where the perp's been looking.'

'Yes,' said West, 'but he's not going to slice open a sofa looking for a locket. He's not going to destroy a divan looking for a locket. And he's certainly not going to rip up the base of a built-in wardrobe looking for a locket. Trust me, he's looking for something bigger.'

'What then?'

'If I knew that, I wouldn't be standing here,' said West as she made her way downstairs, 'I'd be tucking into a bacon double cheeseburger with my feet up. Get on the blower, we need uniform and SOCOs here as soon as possible. Once you've done that, we'll knock up the neighbours and see if anyone saw anything.'

* * *

Resisting the urge to rustle up a slice of toast while Dougal made the call, West leaned against the kitchen units, arms folded, and stared blankly at the floor.

'On the way, miss,' he said. 'Ten minutes, SOCOs to follow.'

'Dougal,' said West quietly. 'Look at the floor.'

'Aye. It's knackered.'

'Yeah I know, but that tile there, by the door, notice anything unusual about it?'

'No. Apart from the fact it's cracked, but then again so are most of them.'

'There's no grout. It's not been sealed properly.'

'Och, it probably went up the hoover, miss.'

'Got a penknife on you?'

'If you're thinking of lifting it, we'll need something a wee bit bigger. I'll see if she has a breadknife about the place.'

Surprised to find the blade disappearing beneath the floor rather than hitting what he expected to be a concrete substrate, Dougal removed the tile in two pieces to reveal a rank, musty-smelling yellow hand towel.

'Oh that's bogging, miss! It needs incinerating!' he said, as he lifted it clear with the tip of the knife. 'Uh-oh, you'd best have a look at this.'

Wearing a self-satisfied grin, West dropped to her knees and eyed a grey, solid steel safe the size of a shoebox lying with the door face-up.

'Like I said, he's looking for something bigger.'

'Well, she's obviously on more than the minimum wage if she's got one of these.'

'Can you lift it out?'

'No chance,' said Dougal. 'It's wedged tight. Will we try the lock?'

'How?' said West. 'We haven't got a key.'

'We don't need one. It's a digital lock and guess what?'

'What?'

'These operate with an alpha-numeric code, anything from six to eight digits.'

'The locket?'

'Aye.'

41

'Be my guest.'

Crouching over the safe, Dougal blew on his fingers and carefully keyed in the numerals 8, 8, 1, 8, followed by two Xs and smiled as the LCD display flashed "open".

'We're in,' he said, grinning like an extra on *The Italian Job*.

'Well, what are you waiting for? Open her up. Let's just hope it's not booby-trapped.'

'Jeez-oh!' said Dougal as the colour drained from his cheeks. 'You don't think…'

'I'm kidding! Get on with it!'

Dougal lifted the door and whistled at the pile of banknotes stashed inside.

'Flipping heck!' said West as she flicked through a bundle of cash bound with a paper sleeve. 'It's full of pinkies.'

'Pinkies?'

'Fifty-pound notes. Let's see, there's about ten grand per bundle so there must be about… a hundred grand here. At least.'

'A hundred thousand! I don't get it,' said Dougal, 'if she's got that much money then why is she not buying herself a nice house, or a decent motor, or…'

'Because, Dougal my lad, she'd have to account for every penny of this to prove it wasn't the proceeds of a robbery or the ill-gotten gains of some money-laundering scam.'

'Which it obviously is,' said Dougal as a blue light bounced off the windows. 'Look sharp. The cavalry's here.'

'Right, you sort them out. I'm going to have a chat with the nosey parker next door.'

* * *

In a remarkable show of self-restraint, West politely jabbed the bell once, stood back, and waited patiently for a reply.

'Detective Inspector West,' she said, flashing her warrant card. Can I have a word?'

An elderly lady wearing a blue, flannelette housecoat and beige tartan slippers regarded her with a xenophobic squint.

'You're not from these parts, are you?' she said.

'No. I'm from London.'

'Is this some kind of international inquiry then?'

'No, madam, I work here. I have done for some time now.'

'Could you not get a job down there?'

'Actually, I prefer it here. Everyone's so... welcoming.'

'Are they indeed?'

'On the whole,' said West, 'yes. Look, I won't keep you long, just a couple of questions about next door.'

'Young Nancy?

'That's right.'

'Has something happened?'

'Nothing to be alarmed about. I just need to know if you've seen anyone hanging around her house recently, say the last twenty-four hours?'

'Not me,' said the lady. 'I'm not one for snooping.'

'Really?'

'Aye. I keep myself to myself.'

'So you didn't see anything?'

'No. Just some fella. He knocked the door.'

'When?'

'Yesterday.'

'Can you remember what time?'

'I'm not a clock-watcher, hen. It was two-thirty.'

'And?'

'She wasn't home.'

'So what did he do?'

'He went around the back.'

'Was he gone long?'

The old lady pursed her lips and shook her head.

'Are you deaf?' she said. 'I've already told you, I'm not a clock-watcher. Twenty-five minutes. Twenty-six maybe.'

'And I don't suppose you remember what he looked like?'

'I do not. Taller than yourself. Slim build. Dark hair, cut short. Very short. And he was wearing a black anorak.'

'I see,' said West. 'Not much to go on, is it? Anything else?'

'No. Just his van. He had a white van. A Mercedes with a trailer hooked to the back.'

* * *

Alone in a car park surrounded by woodland in what appeared to be the middle of nowhere, West – beginning to rue her decision to follow Dougal's directions rather than those of the annoyingly persistent narrator on the sat nav – had no idea where she was or how long it would be before he returned.

Bored by the novelty of watching an irate middle-aged couple struggling to restrain an inquisitive Cairn terrier intent on foraging in the undergrowth, she greeted the buzz of her phone as a welcome distraction.

'Duncan,' she said, stifling a yawn. 'What's up?'

'Result, miss. The CCTV. I think I'm on to something.'

'What have you got?'

'The cleaners. The two Bulgarians. They weren't alone.'

'Go on.'

'It's 7:53 am,' said Duncan. 'They show up as usual and as one of them's opening the door, this fella appears out of nowhere. They have a wee chat, the Bulgarians shrug their shoulders, and he follows them inside.'

'Have you clocked him coming out again?' said West.

'Not yet, miss, but I've only got another half an hour of footage to run through so it's not looking likely.'

'Can you get a make on him?'

'No. I could tell you what he's wearing but it's almost like he's avoiding the camera. I've got a partial on his face in a couple of frames but we need Dougal to look at it, he'll know how to enhance it.'

'Okay, no sweat. He can take a gander as soon as we're back. Anything else?'

'Aye, I'm not sure if it's relevant but there's the front end of a motorcycle just in frame; maybe Dougal can get a match on that too, the model at least, maybe it belongs to the perp'.'

'I'll let him know. So, what are you up to now?'

'I'm going to finish this,' said Duncan, 'then I'm away back up the leisure centre. I'll ask around and see if anyone recognises him by the clothes he was wearing.'

* * *

West, desperate to up her calorie count, checked her watch and fired up the Defender as Dougal hopped into the passenger seat.

'Finally!' she said. 'Where the hell have you been? I thought we were heading for the rugby club.'

'We are,' said Dougal, pointing dead ahead. 'It's just beyond those trees. If we cut through the wood, we'll be right on the pitch.'

'Oh,' said West, killing the engine. 'Why didn't you say so?'

'You didn't ask.'

'Where are we again?'

'Alloway, miss. Millbrae to be precise.'

'So where did you disappear to?'

'That big timber building right behind us.'

'Crikey, if you needed the loo, you should've said.'

'I didn't,' said Dougal, 'it's The Robert Burns Birthplace Museum.'

'Really?'

'Aye, and just over the way there is the Brig O'Doon which is the setting for the final verse in his poem "Tam O'Shanter".'

'No way! So this is where they made that film?'

'No, miss!' said Dougal indignantly. 'The waste of celluloid to which you refer was called *Brigadoon*. It was filmed entirely in America and has absolutely nothing to do with the bridge, or the River Doon, or Ayrshire, or Scottish culture. In fact it has nothing to do with this country at all. Nothing. Zero. Nada. Zilch.'

'I think you've made your point,' said West. 'So why the sudden urge to visit a museum?'

'Oh it wasn't the museum I was after,' said Dougal as he handed her a brown paper bag. 'It was the café. They do a cracking cheese and haggis toastie.'

'Cheese and haggis?' said West. 'No bacon? Or sausage?'

'Try it. You'll not be disappointed.'

Looking as dour as a carnivore tucking into a bowlful of alfalfa sprouts, West tentatively took a bite, savoured it, and licked her lips.

'Blooming heck,' she said. 'You know what? That's really not bad. Not bad at all.'

'We'll make a Scot of you yet,' said Dougal. 'So, will we head for the club?'

* * *

Emerging from the woods, West stood on the touchline, raised her hand to shield her eyes from the low midday sun, and watched a relaxed-looking gent riding a red mower make his way repetitively up and down the pitch.

'That must be him,' said Dougal. 'Jake Nevin.'

'Slim build,' said West. 'Close-cropped hair. Black anorak.'

'Aye, I see that. No need for an audible.'

'It's the description the old biddy gave of Wilson's intruder,' said West.

'Are you joking me? Okay, I have to make a call before we have a chat. We're going to need a car to bring him in.'

Chapter 6

Without a television or Wi-Fi, a mobile phone signal or even a microwave, the isolated cottage on Kilnaughton Bay – with its unfettered view of the ocean to the front and rolling green hills to the rear – offered the perfect retreat for those seeking respite from the rat-race. For others it was a bird-watcher's paradise, and for the few, an ideal location to rest and recuperate after major surgery, but for James Munro, without so much as a crossword to occupy his mind, it was tantamount to a spell in solitary confinement.

Alone on the upper deck with nothing for company but a gentle breeze, he stood quietly contemplating the discovery of one Flora MacDonald as *The Hebridean Isles* glided gently towards Kennacraig until, much to his annoyance, a gaggle of excitable tourists armed with cameras shattered the peace.

Lest he be responsible for the seldom-heard cry of "man overboard", Munro, rankled by their irritatingly inaccurate pronunciation of the island, slipped silently starboard side and pulled his phone from his pocket.

'Duncan,' he said. 'Is that you?'

'Chief! This is a surprise! Are you okay?'

'Aye,' said Munro as a flock of herring gulls squawked overhead. 'Never better.'

'Is it not a bit early to be on the beach?'

'Probably. Listen, is Charlie there?'

'No. She and Dougal are out on a shout, I'm here on my own.'

'Good, because it's you I'm wanting.'

'Me?'

'Aye. Not a word of this to anyone, do I make myself clear?'

'Aye, okay.'

'I'm not on the beach,' said Munro. 'I'm on the boat. We'll be docking in fifteen minutes.'

'The boat? No offence, chief, but have you lost your marbles? You're supposed to be resting.'

'I am, laddie. The best way I know how. Now listen, I need a wee favour.'

'Name it.'

'A laptop. I need a laptop. Is there still a spare one floating about the office?'

'There certainly is,' said Duncan, 'but you'll not be able to access the PNC on it.'

'I'm not needing the National Computer, just the internet.'

'Okey dokey, in that case you're in luck. How will I get it to you?'

'That's the problem,' said Munro. 'I cannae run the risk of bumping into Charlie by coming to the office. Can you meet me in the car park by the shopping centre at three-thirty?'

'Oh, no can do, chief. I've a heap of things to sort out here and if I'm not done by close of play Westy will have my guts for garters.'

'Nae bother, I can wait. How long do you need?'

'I've no idea,' said Duncan. 'Look, how's this; why don't I drop it down to you?'

'To Carsethorn?'

'Aye! You know me, I can do the trip in under an hour. I could be with you for say six o'clock. Seven, maybe.'

'Are you sure?'

'Aye, no danger. You've a four-hour drive ahead of you, you don't want to be hanging around a car park, not in your condition.'

'Well, if you put it like that, then offer accepted.'

'Good. Now if you're wanting the internet, you'll be needing broadband and a router, have they set you up yet?'

'Not yet,' said Munro. 'What with the builders and then the operation I've not had time to arrange it.'

'No worries. I can tether a connection from your phone to the computer and get you online like that.'

'My phone was built in eighteen seventy-two,' said Munro. 'It makes calls, that's it.'

'No bother, we'll use mine.'

'But you'll need it yourself, will you not?'

'Aye I will, but I can hang around for a bit.'

'No, no,' said Munro. 'That's too much to ask.'

'It's fine,' said Duncan. 'I'm meeting Cathy tonight but not until nine o'clock and you'll be in your pit by then, I'm sure. Now, as I'm bringing the laptop is there anything else you're needing? I can fetch it along the way.'

'Well, now that you mention it,' said Munro, 'I've not been home for a while so I'll be needing something for my supper. A steak pie if it's not too much trouble.'

'No trouble at all.'

'From the butcher, mind.'

'Of course.'

'And while you're there, you may as well get some ham and some bacon, and a sirloin for tomorrow. Oh, I'll be needing some teabags too. And some milk. Blue top. And some butter. And a sliced loaf.'

'Is that it?'

'Aye. And some eggs, we'll need eggs. And a decent bottle of red. I'll see you right when you get here.'

* * *

Despite a reprimand as a rookie DC for not following correct police procedure, Duncan – who had an uncanny knack for justifying any means to an end – was not averse to bending the occasional rule and as a consequence completed the trip from Ayr to Carsethorn, with the aid of the flashing blue lights secreted beneath the front grill of the car, in a little under forty minutes.

Startled by the deafening ring of his phone, he cursed under his breath and slew to a halt outside the Steamboat Inn to take the call he'd been dreading.

'Miss,' he said, trying his best to sound out of breath. 'How's tricks?'

'All good,' said West, 'we're just back in the office. We've arrested that bloke Nancy Wilson was dating on suspicion of breaking and entering.'

'Oh no, does that mean we've a long night ahead of us?'

'Not if I can help it. He's a stroppy so-and-so, so I'm going to let him stew overnight, we'll question him tomorrow. Where are you?'

'Oh, I'm just leaving the leisure centre,' said Duncan. 'I've asked around but no-one recognises the fella from the description I gave.'

'Then it's my guess,' said West, 'that after blagging his way past the Bulgarians he found a cosy, little hidey-hole and lay low until closing time.'

'Aye, my thoughts exactly,' said Duncan. 'Incidentally, miss, I've left my laptop open with the CCTV paused at the point where the cleaners turn up. If Dougal wants to take a look, it's the fella in blue jeans and a black anorak he's looking for.'

'Okay,' said West, 'I'll let him… hold up! Black anorak you say?'

'Aye, and he's got the hood up.'

'Well, well, well. Looks like our guest is about to have another charge thrown at him.'

'How so?'

'I'll explain later. How long will it take you to get back?'

Duncan took a deep breath, ran a hand through his unruly mop of hair, and gritted his teeth.

'The thing is, miss,' he said, 'I'm on a promise tonight so I was kind of hoping…'

'Yeah, yeah. No sweat. You go enjoy yourself but no hangovers, right? I want you here early. Dougal's going to be tied up and I need a background check on this Jake Nevin geezer before we interview him.'

'Roger that, miss. I'll be there.'

Justifying the white lie as an excusable offence on the grounds that his journey south was, in the absence of a supermarket home delivery service, a mercy dash to save someone less able than himself from the imminent threat of starvation, Duncan gave a wry smile, fired up the engine and crawled the final hundred yards to Munro's cottage. A soft yellow light glowed in the window and plumes of grey smoke billowed from the chimney against a darkening sky.

'The door was open, chief!' he said as he dumped the carrier bags on the floor. 'They've made a good job of the house, you'd never guess the back end was blown to pieces.'

'That's the beauty of gas,' said Munro. 'Controllable but flammable in the extreme. Not unlike yourself. Take a seat, I'm just pokering up the fire.'

'No, you're alright. First things first, I'll get these groceries away and stick the kettle on.'

'Tea o'clock has been and gone,' said Munro. 'I'll take a glass of wine, if you've remembered to bring a bottle.'

'I have indeed,' said Duncan as he placed it on the table. 'It's a Côtes du Rhône, twelve percent. Will that do you?'

'Perfectly. Will you take a glass?'

'Not for me, thanks chief, I'm driving. Are you okay? You're looking awful peely-wally.'

'I'm fine, laddie, just hungry. I was about to put some soup on the hob but it's not the same without a slice or two.'

'Well, I'll get this stuff in the fridge and rustle something up. Are you still wanting soup or will I stick the pie in the oven?'

'I'll have the pie please,' said Munro, 'and there's a tin of baked beans in the cupboard.'

Lovingly restored to its former glory, the kitchen – with its Belfast sink, box sash windows and handmade units – was, bar a few spots of "Wimborne White" on the timber floor and a rock-hard paintbrush sitting on the counter, worthy of a spread in Homes and Gardens magazine.

'There's a wee mess in here, chief,' said Duncan. 'If you've got some white spirit, I'll give it a quick wipe down.'

'As it happens, I've a bottle of turpentine in my coat pocket; I'll fetch it for you now.'

* * *

Munro, conveniently heeding the doctor's advice to keep physical exertion to a minimum for the first time since being discharged from hospital, sipped his wine and smiled appreciatively as Duncan wiped the paint from the floor and set the brush in a glass of turps.

'If Westy finds out I'm here,' he said, 'she'll blow a fuse.'

'She'll not find out, not unless you open your trap.'

'Oh, I'm saying nothing but you know what she's like, and it's not just me who'll feel the sharp side of her tongue – you'll be for the high jump too.'

'How so?'

'The cottage. She paid a wee fortune for that place on Islay and you jumped ship a week early.'

'Oh aye, so I did. I'll give her a call in the morning and let her know I'm back.'

'Aye, probably best. Right, where do you want the computer?'

'On the table by the fire, please.'

Munro took a seat, pulled on his spectacles, and placed his notebook alongside the laptop while Duncan configured the connection to his phone.

'Right, that's you,' he said. 'What is it you're looking for, chief, if you don't mind me asking?'

'Nothing exciting,' said Munro. 'Just some research is all.'

'Oh aye?'

'An elderly lady by the name of MacDonald disappeared some years ago. She was the wife of the village postmaster and now she's turned up out of the blue.'

'So was she away on her holidays or something?'

'Not quite,' said Munro. 'It appears she got herself into a bit of a squeeze. A tight spot, you might say.'

'You've lost me.'

'She was found up a chimney. In her own home.'

'Dear, dear,' said Duncan shaking his head, 'that's no way to go, is it? Even so, I'm not being morbid mind, but it sounds like the kind of thing I'd love to have a crack at.'

'I'm sure you would,' said Munro, 'but unfortunately for you, you are Ayrshire and this is in the hands of Dumfries and Galloway.'

'Pity. Right, I'll fetch your pie while you crack on. Are you wanting your beans hot or cold?'

'Cold? Dear, dear, I never had you down as a heathen, laddie. Hot, of course, by which I mean piping. There's a saucepan on the shelf and you'll be joining me, there's enough for two.'

* * *

With the dexterity of an arthritic pianist playing a less than accomplished rendition of "Chopsticks", Munro – who embraced technology with the zeal of a Luddite – stabbed the keyboard with the forefingers of both hands while Duncan, refraining from interfering, polished off his supper in silence.

'I'll clear these away,' he said, collecting the plates. 'Are you wanting a pudding?'

Munro looked up, removed his spectacles, and rubbed his eyes.

'Aye,' he said, yawning as he made his way to the sofa. 'Whisky. The Balvenie's on the sideboard. I think I need to rest a while.'

'I'm not surprised,' said Duncan. 'You've had a day of it.'

'Och, it's not so much the travelling, it's that blessed screen. How on earth do folk these days stare at those things without going blind?'

'They do,' said Duncan. 'Well, near enough. Guaranteed they're all wearing glasses before they reach thirty and then they complain that their human rights were violated because they weren't warned of the dangers of working with computers.'

'Utter tosh.'

'Agreed, but that's millennials for you, chief. The snowflakes. They're as soft as fudge and they think the world owes them a living.'

'I wouldnae worry if I were you,' said Munro. 'You know what happens to a snowflake when you turn up the heat.'

'Right enough,' said Duncan. 'Okay, I'll get these dishes washed and then…'

'Och, not necessary, laddie, leave them where they are. Is there not somewhere you have to be?'

'I've time yet. Just you relax.'

As unofficial stepfather to his girlfriend's eleven-year-old son, Duncan was used to making Cameron as comfortable as possible when he collapsed with exhaustion after a weekend's rambling, mountain biking, or beachcombing, but there was something unsettlingly palliative about applying the same degree of compassionate care to a retired police officer.

Wary of waking a dozing Munro, he carefully draped a woollen blanket across his chest, returned to the table and poured himself a glass of red before sending Cathy an apologetic text and settling in front of the computer to browse the search history and Munro's barely legible notes.

* * *

Like a beleaguered walrus beset by coltish calves, Munro snarled and snorted as he woke from his slumber, took a moment to reacquaint himself with his surroundings, and eyed Duncan with a shallow look of confusion.

'Sorry,' he said, discarding the blanket. 'I must have dropped off for a few minutes.'

'Aye, so you did.'

'You'd best take yourself off or you'll be late. What time is it?'

'Nearly four.'

'Four! Four o'clock? In the morning?'

'Aye.'

'By jiminy! Why didn't you wake me?'

'You know what they say about sleeping dogs.'

'But you had a date!' said Munro. 'With your lady friend.'

'Had, chief. Past tense. She blew me out. Now, do you fancy a brew?'

'Aye, that would be most welcome, laddie. Most welcome indeed.'

Duncan returned from the kitchen with two mugs of steaming hot tea and a plate of toast and marmalade.

'Have you not slept?' said Munro, warming his hands on the mug.

'No, chief. I've been busy.'

'How so?'

'Well, I had to keep the fire going,' said Duncan, 'so you didn't catch a chill and... I took a look at your searches on the internet. I hope I've not overstepped the mark.'

'No skin off my nose, laddie.'

'And I read your notes.'

'You have been busy.'

'And I found a few things you might like to see. Will I show you?'

Munro finished his toast, took a large swig of tea, and joined Duncan at the table.

'Okay,' he said. 'Let's have it.'

'If you're sure, but if I'm barking up the wrong tree just tell me to shut my hole and I'll pass it back to you. Let's start with this fella you've been looking for: Craig McPherson.'

'The amateur boxer.'

'Is that what he was? Well, that would explain his behaviour then.'

'In what way?'

'I found an article in the archives of the Galloway Gazette; a fella by the name of McPherson was cautioned for causing a disturbance at the Bruce Hotel in Newton Stewart years ago and guess what, it was the day after Flora MacDonald was reported missing.'

'What kind of a disturbance?'

'Seems he was lording it up,' said Duncan. 'He'd stopped for two nights, during which time he was spending cash like it was going out of fashion, getting hammered, and picking fights with anyone who'd take him on.'

'So he fancied himself as a wee hard man after all.'

'Maybe, but he was nothing of the sort. He got floored by every one of his opponents, including the barmaid.'

Munro sat back, folded his arms, and stared pensively at the ceiling.

'McPherson lived in Palnackie,' he said. 'And the Bruce Hotel is in Newton Stewart. If he only stopped the two nights, then where was he going? Why was he travelling west?'

'Search me,' said Duncan, 'there's nothing out that way but Stranraer.'

'The port?'

'Aye. Oh! If he did have something to do with that old lady dying then maybe he was legging it – he could have jumped the boat to Belfast or Dublin even.'

'You might be on to something there,' said Munro. 'We'll have to contact the ferry company and ask if they still have a copy of the manifest for all the sailings the following day.'

'We?'

'I mean me.'

'Aye. Of course you do,' said Duncan. 'Let's move on. This other fella, Archibald Galbraith. He's the head teacher at the school in Palnackie, has been for years, and he's also on the parish council.'

'Tell me something I havenae heard.'

'Okay, chief, I'll try. A few years back, Galbraith campaigned vociferously for new facilities at the school claiming the place was over-crowded. He said that the cramped conditions were, quote, "*not fit for a sustained period of successful education and having a detrimental effect on the well-being of the students*" and he got the support of the entire community. Eventually the council caved in and agreed to fund the construction of two eco-friendly, modular classrooms. The project was put out to tender but here's the thing – the company which landed the contract, Caisteal Estates, was the one with the highest bid.'

'Is that so?'

'In fact they were three times more than their nearest rival.'

'Well, perhaps they were a better outfit,' said Munro. 'Reputable, using better quality materials and employing qualified craftsmen.'

'That's not the case, chief. If you Google images of the school, you'll see the new build's falling apart. I'd say it was built to budget, a tiny wee budget.'

'Let's go back a step,' said Munro. 'If their quote was so high then surely they'd have fallen at the first hurdle and been dismissed out of court. Did no-one oppose it?'

'Aye, they did. Unanimously. The general consensus was that the council should be saving money and not frittering it away, but it was all rubber-stamped and pushed through regardless.'

'And how do you know all this?'

'FOI,' said Duncan. 'I found a Freedom of Information request directed at the council asking them for details of the costs.'

'So, what's the story?' said Munro. 'There has to be a reason for paying these folk over the odds for completing the project.'

'There is. And you're going to love it. The person with the final say-so in the planning department was a lady by the name of Lucinda Mulqueen. She was the one who signed the cheque, so to speak.'

'Go on.'

'She was also head of the parent-teacher association at the school.'

'Interesting but not exactly riveting.'

'Maybe not,' said Duncan as he spun the laptop to face Munro, 'but this is. What you're looking at here is the Companies House website. Caisteal Estates was set up just two weeks before the contract went out to tender and get this, it folded less than a month after the work was completed.'

'I smell something akin to rat,' said Munro as he finished his tea. 'Now go easy, laddie, I cannae afford to raise my blood pressure too much.'

'Scroll down the page, chief. You'll see a list of Caisteal Estates' board of directors – Lucinda Alice Mulqueen and Archibald Alpin Galbraith – but that's not the best bit. The company secretary was one Jack MacDonald.'

'Jumping Jehoshaphat!' said Munro. 'MacDonald! Why, he was the postmaster!'

'Take it easy, chief. Will I fetch you an aspirin?'

'No, no. It would appear there may be a link then, between these shenanigans and the demise of Flora MacDonald.'

'It's possible,' said Duncan. 'I cross-checked with Births, Marriages, and Deaths. Jack MacDonald passed away five weeks after Caisteal went out of business.'

Munro hauled himself from his chair, walked to the window and stared out to sea as the sun broke over the horizon, his hands clasped firmly behind his back.

'Five weeks,' he said. 'Just long enough for him to get his hands on his slice of the profits.'

'Profits? I'm not with you, chief.'

'Dear God!' said Munro, 'you're letting yourself down! How on earth can you turn in an exemplary performance like that and forget the punch line? Do you not see it? Galbraith and his cohorts knew the project was coming up for tender so they formed the company, used Mulqueen to push their bid through, then completed the build as cheaply as possible, syphoning off the balance to line their own pockets.'

'I didn't see that coming,' said Duncan as he ruffled his hair. 'Must be fatigue setting in.'

'Charlie will hear of this, laddie. Mark my words, your efforts will not be without reward.'

'Oh no, chief, I'm not sure that's such a good...'

'Wheesht! It's not for you to say. Now, let's put the icing on the cake. Have you any figures?'

'Aye, they're here somewhere, chief, in the FOI I think but I've not got time to look just now, I need to get a shift on.'

'Pity,' said Munro. 'I was in mind of a wee celebration.'

'Are you joking me? I'm not touching the booze, not at this time of the morning!'

'Who said anything about booze? I was thinking eggs, bacon, and a fried slice.'

'Tempting, chief,' said Duncan, 'but I'll have to take a rain check. If I'm not in the office by six, Westy's going to kill me.'

'As you wish, laddie. You've done more than enough here and for that I'm grateful.'

'No bother, and listen, if you can't find those figures then give me a call, on the mobile mind, and I'll take a look when I get a wee moment to myself.'

Chapter 7

After a turbulent two years under the repressive gaze of a blue-blooded libertine well-versed in the art of coercion, during which time she'd feared for her mental health, West – enjoying a hitherto unseen state of emotional stability – was shrewd enough to acknowledge, in his absence, that were it not for Munro's derisive sarcasm and dogged determination to get her career back on track, she would have remained in London, surrounded by misogynistic colleagues, with nothing to look forward to after her shift but a bucket of fried chicken and a bottle of cheap vodka. Moreover, she was in no doubt that had she not followed her mentor north to Caledonia she would have relinquished her role as a DS within weeks of his departure and sprinted down a path of self-destruction.

Perturbed by the fact that he'd yet to return any of her calls, and growing increasingly concerned that he may have suffered a relapse, she drafted a hasty email for her colleagues on Islay to request that they visit the holiday home on Kilnaughton Bay as soon as possible, preferably with a paramedic in tow.

Unable to concentrate further, not least because of Munro's seemingly selfish attitude, she abandoned her frustratingly fruitless search for any snippet of information on the untraceable Jake Nevin, closed the laptop, and fell sound asleep on the sofa.

Startled by the ear-splitting screech of her phone at 5 am – a time traditionally reserved for the conveyance of news concerning the demise of a close relative – she fell to the floor and anxiously retrieved an apologetic voicemail from a typically droll Munro, informing her of his intention to call once he'd completed a relaxing session of tantric yoga and polished off a bowl of vitamin-rich organic muesli, muscle injuries and gastroenteritis notwithstanding. Relieved to know that he wasn't lying under a sheet in the chiller cabinet at University Hospital, she checked her watch, demolished the remnants of a family-sized bar of milk chocolate, and readied herself for work.

* * *

Whilst the sight of a blackened body lying in the smouldering remains of a burned-out bungalow was as unsettling to behold as the hollow eyes of a dead drug addict, it was, more often than not, the surprisingly mundane discoveries which harboured an innate ability to consistently shock; like a spider the size of Finland lurking beneath the sink, a discarded doll skulking in the closet, or the sight of DC Duncan Reid alone in a darkened office at 5:48 am.

'Flipping heck!' said West. 'You look like death.'

'You're not bad yourself.'

'What are you doing here so early?'

'I couldn't sleep,' said Duncan, the bags under his eyes accentuated by the cool, blue glow of his computer screen, 'so I thought I'd crack on with the background check.'

'Best of luck,' said West. 'I spent hours searching for something on that Jake Nevin geezer last night and I couldn't find a thing.'

'You were looking for the wrong fella.'

'Come again?'

'Jake. It's a pet name for John. It's John Nevin you should've been looking for.'

'Now he tells me. Did you find anything?'

'Plenty,' said Duncan. 'I've typed up a crib sheet and left it on your desk.'

'Blimey, slow down, mate. You're turning into a right little swot, you know that?'

'I aim to please.'

'Is there anything I should know about right now?'

'That all depends on what you're looking for,' said Duncan. 'He lives on Church Street, that's about a six-minute walk from Nancy Wilson. He's forty-nine years old, single, and he lives alone. And according to the business card he carries in his wallet, he's a professional groundsman...'

'Now that, I do know.'

'...but I reckon he's pulling a fast one.'

'Why?'

'Because he's registered unemployed. He's on the social.'

'Is he indeed?'

'And he's claiming housing too which means every penny he earns from cutting the grass goes into his back pocket undeclared.'

'Well, I hope he's put some by,' said West, 'because that's a shedload of benefits he's going to have to pay back. Anything else?'

Duncan swung his feet onto the table, leaned back, and ran his fingers through his hair.

'There is,' he said with a knowing smile. 'And it's a beauty.'

'Go on.'

'He's got previous. Six years ago, he was done for aggravated assault. He pummelled the living daylights out of his ex.'

'I'm beginning to like this.'

'He got two years; six months suspended.'

'So, he likes knocking women about, does he? Just wait until I'm finished with him. Why did he do it?'

'Lost his temper,' said Duncan. 'A one-off. Apparently.'

'Yeah, right. Do we know who she is?'

'We do indeed. A Miss Kate Murray.'

'Miss? So they weren't married?'

'No, and get this,' said Duncan, 'according to her statement, they'd only been seeing each other a few weeks. She moved away after his conviction.'

'Can't blame her for that,' said West. 'Where is she now?'

'Hamilton.'

'And where's that?'

'Glasgow, near enough. Will I give her a call?'

'Better had,' said West, 'we haven't got time to go traipsing all the way up there. Oh, and when you've done that, I need you to nip over to Nevin's place and give it the once over. His keys are with the rest of his stuff.'

'Roger that,' said Duncan. 'Do we have a warrant?'

'We will have when Dougal sorts one out, but don't let a little thing like that hold you up. Now, for being so… what's the word?'

'Clever? Talented? Compassionate? Caring?'

'I was thinking *industrious*. For being so industrious, I'm going to treat you to breakfast. You stick the kettle on while I pop to the café, what do you want?'

'Oh, I'll have the full works please. Thanks very much.'

'Sorry,' said West, 'you'll have to make do with a roll for now, I want to interview Nevin as soon as Dougal gets here and you've got work to do.'

'Fair enough, but if Dougal's not here by the time you get back, I get his by default, okay?'

'Get my what?' said Dougal as he breezed through the door. 'Jeez-oh! What are you doing here? Have you been on the Red Bull again?'

'Very funny.'

'Well, do you know what time it is? Should you not be in your pit?'

'I'll dig one for you if you're not careful. What's in the bag?'

'Breakfast,' said Dougal. 'As usual, one sausage and one bacon.'

'Smashing.'

'But I wasn't expecting to see you here, so I've only brought the two.'

'That'll do me.'

'Give him mine,' said West, 'he's earned it. Just make sure there's a tea on the go by the time I get back.'

As someone who ranked suspicion above trust in the league of interpersonal skills, Dougal, intrigued by Duncan's untimely presence in the office, filled the kettle, tossed him a toastie, and pulled up a chair.

'*You've earned it*,' he said, eyeing him with an inquisitive tilt of the head. 'What did she mean by that?'

'No idea, pal.'

'Well, there has to be a reason. I mean, why are you here so early?'

'Couldn't sleep.'

'No, no,' said Dougal. 'That's not it. See here, in all the time we've worked together I have never seen you in the office before me, let alone with West, it just doesn't... oh hold on now! Just a minute! Don't tell me you and she have been...'

'Away and chase yourself!' said Duncan, choking on his sandwich. 'Have you lost the plot? Of course we have not!'

'Well, what is it then? Was it an all-nighter with Cathy? Have you two been arguing? Or is it the wean, is he not well?'

Duncan scowled across the desk, dusted the crumbs from his fingers, and grabbed his coat.

'You need to keep this,' he said, tapping the side of his nose, 'out of other folk's business.'

'No offence, I was only trying to help.'

'Is that so? Well, just you remember what happened to the curious cat, okay? Now, if it's all the same with you, I'm away to see what Nevin's got stashed beneath his bed. You'll find his back-story on the desk.'

'So that's what you've been doing! You should've said. Look, apologies okay? I shouldn't have jumped to conclusions.'

'Get over it,' said Duncan. 'I have. Oh, and a word to the wise, this Nevin fella's handy with his fists so I'd sit behind Westy if I were you.'

* * *

Devoid of residents rushing to work or children dallying on their way to school, the only thing missing from a deserted Church Street, apart from a pulse, was a token ball of tumbleweed blowing across the pavement.

Reminiscent of the housing scheme where he himself was raised, Duncan, aware that most of the tenants had neither the will nor the need to leave their homes until hunger drove them from their beds, cruised past the row of lifeless houses until he reached Nevin's shambolic end-of-terrace bordered by an overgrown hedge with a garage to one side and a decommissioned satellite dish dangling precariously by a cable above the front door.

Looking like any one of the ten-a-penny miscreants who frequented the area, he slinked up the path and slipped unnoticed into the house where, unfazed by the damp floorboards, the peeling paintwork, and the stench of stale beer, he paused for a cursory glance of the lounge before making his way to the kitchen, where a pile of bin bags lay festering beneath the worktop in a space once occupied by a washing machine and a refrigerator.

With the hob covered in enough grease to lubricate the wheels of a ten tonne artic and a frying pan coated in a white layer of congealed fat, he assumed Nevin to have a cholesterol count of 9.2, turned on his heels, and scooted upstairs to sneer at his sleeping arrangements which, judging by the stained mattress lying on the floor and the mounds of soiled laundry scattered about the room, had more in common with a vagrant's makeshift bed in the recess of a shop doorway than a haven of peace and tranquillity.

Avoiding the bathroom on the grounds of health and safety, Duncan peered inside the box room and, hoping that his superior wasn't already in the throes of an in-depth interview, reached for his phone.

'Duncan,' said West. 'Make it quick, I'm on my way downstairs.'

'I'm at Nevin's house, miss. Tell me something, is the male of the species genetically hard-wired to forget about cleaning when he hits forty?'

'What the hell are you gabbing on about?'

'This Nevin fella and Rupert Lea, they're peas in a pod. Pigs, the pair of them.'

'Get to the point!'

'Sorry. The place is a flea pit, trust me it's toxic; it should be condemned but there's something a wee bit weird going on here.'

West, sensing the ripple of butterflies in her stomach, paused on the landing.

'Go on,' she said. 'This had better be good.'

'Okay, the whole house is falling apart except for the wee bedroom at the back of the house. It's immaculate, I mean spotless, you could eat off the floor. There's a spanking new wardrobe, a single bed with clean sheets and even a pair of flowery curtains.'

'Well, maybe he's just started decorating.'

'No, no,' said Duncan impatiently, 'he's definitely not decorating. Nevin's nearly fifty years old, he's single and he lives alone, right?'

'Right?'

'But the room's been painted this soft, baby blue.'

'Okay, not very masculine I grant you but…'

'But here's the creepy thing,' said Duncan, 'there's a jug of fresh flowers on the bedside table, a teddy bear in the bed, a big poster of Winnie-the-Pooh on the wall, and a mobile hanging from the light with these sort of Disney characters on it.'

'So, what are you saying?'

'I'm saying we need to do another check on Nevin, and quick,' said Duncan. 'We need to know if he's got any kids, or nieces, or nephews.'

'And if he hasn't?'

'Well, if he hasn't, miss, then I reckon there's every chance we've got a nonce on our hands.'

* * *

Having spent the best part of thirty-five years working alone, Jake Nevin – ex-road sweeper, labourer, roofer, farmhand, caretaker, and courier – did not crave the companionship of his fellow man, nor did he hanker after the idle small talk that accompanied a pie and a pint in his local. Instead he preferred to dine alone, drink alone, and sleep alone, despite the fact that there was, and had been for some years, something intangible missing from his life.

Unable to afford a lawyer, and neither eloquent nor articulate enough to defend himself against a possible charge of breaking and entering, Nevin nonetheless declined his right to a duty solicitor on the basis that he could not claim to be entirely innocent of any iniquitous activities and hoped instead that a guileless response to any probing questions would be enough to acquit him of any wrong doing.

Perched on the edge of his seat with his hands clasped between his knees, he locked eyes with West and mustered a half-hearted smile as Dougal, wary of provoking the pint-sized Popeye too much, gently pressed the record button.

'For the benefit of the tape,' he said, 'I am DS McCrae, also present is Detective Inspector West. Would you state your name, please?'

'Jake Nevin.'

'And where do you stay, Mr Nevin?'

'Auchinleck. Church Street.'

'Do you understand why you're here?'

'Not really,' said Nevin. 'You seem to think I robbed somebody's house. Is that it?'

'Pretty much,' said West, 'but the thing is, it's not just anybody's house we're talking about, is it? It's Nancy Wilson's.'

'Nancy! Are you joking me? Why would I want to rob her?'

'You tell me.'

'She never mentioned it. If she had then maybe I could've helped.'

'Yes, I'm sure you could.'

'Is she okay?' said Nevin. 'I mean, was she there when they broke in? Was she hurt?'

'I've got to hand it to you, Mr Nevin,' said West, smirking as she folded her arms, 'you're turning in a great performance.'

'I'm not with you. What do you mean, *a great performance*?'

'Nancy Wilson,' said Dougal abruptly. 'She's dead.'

Nevin, his brow as furrowed as a freshly ploughed field, sat up with a jolt.

'Dead?' he said, his voice as soft as a whisper. 'But how can that be?'

West smiled and shrugged her shoulders.

'You're confusing me,' he said, 'I mean she was as fit as fiddle. Was it her heart, is that it? Did her heart give out?'

'Aye,' said Dougal, 'that and a few other things. Tell me, Mr Nevin, have you been in a brawl recently?'

'A brawl? No, no. I'm not one for trouble, why?'

'The scratches on your neck, they look nasty.'

'One of the perils of the job,' said Nevin. 'Hawthorn. Wee jaggy branches. It's like cutting back razor blades.'

'You should be more careful. So, when was the last time you saw Miss Wilson exactly?'

'Christ, now you're asking. I don't know. I can't say for sure, a few days ago, I think; no, a week maybe.'

'And where was that?'

'At the leisure centre of course.'

'Why *of course*,' said West. 'I mean, it could've been anywhere. The pub, a restaurant. Your house. Hers. After all, the two of you were seeing each other, were you not?'

'Well, aye,' said Nevin nervously, 'but not seriously, it's not like we were in a relationship. We'd been out together a couple of times but that was it.'

'Don't tell me, it didn't work out.'

'No. It did not.'

'How so?' said Dougal. 'You two seem pretty compatible to me; both in similar lines of work, both with a love of the outdoors, you're even of a similar age.'

'Hardly,' said Nevin. 'I've a few years on her.'

'So, who called it off?' said West. 'You or Nancy?'

'Nancy.'

'Why?'

'She never said, but I got the feeling she probably didn't think I was smart enough for her, and she'd have been right.'

'How very humble of you,' said West. 'So even though she blew you out, you still continued to see each other.'

'We did, aye. What with work and such, it was unavoidable.'

'And the two of you were okay together? No sour grapes? No animosity?'

'No, none. We carried on as normal.'

'Describe normal.'

'We were pals,' said Nevin. 'Friends. Good friends. We were polite and civil to each other. We'd share a joke or have a wee chat over a cup of coffee, that sort of thing.'

Dougal fired up his laptop, put it to one side and, hand on chin, regarded Nevin inquisitively.

'If you had a job to do at the centre,' he said, 'did you ever have reason to arrive early?'

'Early?'

'Aye. Like half six in the morning, seven o'clock maybe?'

'Seven? No way. Never.'

'So you're not an early riser then?' said West.

'It's not that,' said Nevin. 'It's the dew. It's never good to cut the grass when it's heavy with dew, it's best to let it dry off. Often by midday I'm good to go.'

'Then why were you there at 7:53 am?'

'Not me, sorry. Why would I arrive that early?'

'So you could nip in unnoticed and take care of Nancy.'

'Take care of her?'

'That's where she was murdered.'

'Murdered? Dear God! You said she was dead!'

'Six of one,' said West, 'whichever way you look at it, the result's the same.'

'Jesus! She didn't deserve that! Why? Why would anyone want to murder Nancy?'

'That's what we're trying to find out.'

'So this is not about a burglary then, this is… hold on now, just a minute! You think that I…? Listen, I would never hurt Nancy. Never. She's lovely. She's the loveliest girl I've met in a long time!'

Dougal spun his laptop round to face Nevin.

'For the benefit of the tape, I am now showing Mr Nevin CCTV footage taken from outside the leisure centre where a figure matching Mr Nevin's description can be seen talking to the cleaners as they arrive, before entering the building unchallenged on the day of Miss Wilson's death.'

'It's the same anorak,' said Nevin, 'I'll give you that.'

'And the same jeans,' said Dougal. 'And the same boots.'

'Aye okay, but I'm telling you, that's not me!'

West stared at Nevin, held his gaze, then stood and ambled towards the rear of the room.

'Have you been in trouble before?' she said. 'Have you ever been arrested? Or charged?'

Nevin craned his neck in an effort to see her and cleared his throat.

'I have,' he said ashamedly. 'Once or twice. As a wean.'

'As a wean?'

'Aye, you know, pinching sweeties from the supermarket, lifting the odd pushbike here and there. Kids' stuff, really.'

'Kids' stuff? I wouldn't call aggravated assault kids' stuff, would you?'

Nevin hung his head and ran his hands over his bristly hair.

'I'm not proud of it,' he said quietly. 'Not proud at all.'

'The thing is,' said West, 'the person you belted wasn't some bloke in the pub, was it? It wasn't some thug on the terraces at a football match. It was a woman, and from where I'm standing I'd say that was grossly unfair, considering your size.'

'I'm five-foot six,' said Nevin. 'Not exactly the Jolly Green Giant.'

'I'm not talking about your height, Mr Nevin. Look at you. You look as though you've overdosed on steroids.'

'I like to keep in shape.'

'So, what happened?' said Dougal. 'Why did you wallop that girl?'

'Because she wound me up. I lost my temper.'

'So you've got a short fuse?'

'No.'

'Then you harbour grudges, is that it? Or is it because you felt belittled because, just like Nancy Wilson, she dumped you too?'

* * *

Beginning to wish he'd accepted the offer of legal aid after all, Nevin squirmed in his seat as Dougal, alerted to a call from Duncan, glanced at West, raised two fingers, and stood.

'For the benefit of the tape,' she said, 'DS McCrae has left the room to take a telephone call. Have you got any family, Mr Nevin? Any brothers or sisters? Any kids?'

'No. No family.'

'So you don't have many visitors then? No friends dropping by? No nieces or nephews having a sleep-over?'

'No. Like I said. None. My father passed away last year so that's it now. It's just me, on my own.'

'Shame,' said West. 'It must be lonely for you.'

'Sometimes,' said Nevin, 'but I'm not without hope. You never know what's around the corner.'

'No, you certainly don't. Do you like reading, Mr Nevin?'

'Not really.'

'So you're not a fan of, say, A.A. Milne?'

'Never heard of him.'

'What about TV? What do you like watching? Drama? Documentaries? Or cartoons?'

'I'm not with you.'

West paused as Dougal, trying his utmost not to smile, returned to his seat, leaned across the table, and glared at Nevin.

'Let's go back a bit,' he said. 'Let's talk about the assault. You got two years for that so it must've been quite a beating you gave the young lady, am I right?'

'It was a one-off,' said Nevin. 'I didn't mean it.'

'Of course you didn't. And the lady in question, she was...?'

'Kate. Kate Murray.'

'Aye. Kate Murray. And she was your girlfriend, was she not?'

'Not so much a girlfriend, more a...'

'More a what?' said West, hackles raised. 'A one-night stand? Another notch on your bedpost?'

'It was mutual,' said Nevin, 'casual. It's not as if I forced her into something she didn't want to do.'

'Then why did you hit her?'

'I told you, I lost my temper.'

'Aye, we know that!' said Dougal, raising his voice, 'but there has to be a reason. Was it because she burned your supper? No, probably not. Was it because she spilled your beer? Aye, could be. Or was it because she was pregnant? Surely not, because that would never do, would it? Hitting a pregnant lady?'

Nevin locked his hands together and cracked his knuckles.

'It was a shock,' he said, 'we'd only been seeing each other a couple of weeks and...'

'And naturally it was her fault!' said West. 'It was her fault she got pregnant!'

'See here, Mr Nevin, we've spoken to Miss Murray and she tells us you went after her on bended knee,' said Dougal, 'pleading forgiveness, pleading to see your wee boy, and that's why you've got your spare room done up like a nursery, isn't it? In the hope that he'd come visit; only she told you where to go, didn't she?'

'Pity really,' said West, 'because if he had visited then you could've been claiming child support as well as the dole, and housing. You'd have been raking it in.'

'Are you going to do me for that?' said Nevin. 'For claiming benefits?'

'It's fraud, Mr Nevin. And I'm going to do you for everything I can.'

'But there's no way I can afford to pay that back.'

'You should've thought about that before you decided to keep quiet about your job.'

'Look, I didn't tell anyone about the job or the bairn because if I did, I'd have to pay child maintenance and I don't have two pennies to rub together.'

'How so?' said Dougal. 'I mean, you must earn a fair bit riding around on that mower of yours.'

'I do, aye. A wee bit. And I put it aside for the bairn.'

'Well, unless you can prove it,' said Dougal, 'you're humped, Mr Nevin. Well and truly.'

'Let me tell you where I am,' said West. 'We've got you on CCTV outside the leisure centre the morning of Miss Wilson's death…'

'That's not me.'

'…plus you've got a history of violence against women…'

'It was a one off! A stupid mistake!'

'…and not only that, we've got a witness who'll testify to seeing you loitering around Miss Wilson's house just hours after she was killed, so guess what? We're going to hold you a little bit longer.'

'But why?' said Nevin. 'For benefit fraud? For breaking and entering?'

'No, no,' said Dougal. 'We're holding you on suspicion of the murder of Nancy Wilson but look on the bright side, we're not charging you, not just yet. In the meantime, for the purposes of DNA profiling, we'll need a swab from inside your cheek and as you've obviously not changed your clothes for a couple of days, we'll have those too.'

'Come on,' said West. 'Back in your box and get your kit off. Someone will bring you a lovely little boiler suit to wear until we get your clothes back.'

Chapter 8

Sensing none of the euphoria she'd experienced on previous cases when, hard evidence aside, she'd naively assumed the facts alone would have been enough to secure a conviction, West, looking unusually dour, sat staring silently into space with a slice of pepperoni pizza dangling from one hand and a spicy chicken wing in the other.

'Are you okay?' said Dougal, concerned by her sullen expression.

'Sorry? What was that?'

'Are you sickening for something, miss? Your lunch, you've not touched it.'

'Nah, not that hungry really.'

'Oh dear. Oh dear, dear, dear.'

'What's that supposed to mean?'

'You and food,' said Dougal, 'it's not right. It's not right at all. No offence, miss, but when my doggie stopped eating, I knew something was up. Six weeks later he was dead.'

'Thanks for that.'

'So, what is it?'

'I'm having doubts,' said West.

'About Nevin?'

'Yup.'

'But why? He ticks all the boxes.'

'I know,' said West, 'but there's something about him, he's just not… he's just not demented enough.'

'Well, they say it's the quiet ones you have to look out for.'

'I know, but he's not your stereotypical nine-to-fiver nice guy with a barrel-load of mates and twelve choirboys chained to the wall in his cellar, is he?'

'No,' said Dougal as he answered the phone, 'maybe not. So, what do you think?'

'My head says we bide our time and wait for the results from forensics, but my instinct says he's in the clear.'

Dougal held the handset to his chest and spoke in a loud whisper.

'No need to fret,' he said. 'I think you just got yourself a second bite of the cherry.'

'You what?'

'Rupert Lea. The lads in Cumnock have picked him up.'

'Hallelujah!' said West. 'About time too! Tell them to stick him in a car and send him here now.'

'That's if he agrees to come.'

'Well, why wouldn't he? Hold on, when you say they picked him up, did they arrest him or…'

'No, no,' said Dougal. 'They asked if he'd care to help with the inquiry and he went of his own accord.'

'Bugger.'

'Is that not good?'

'I don't know,' said West. 'Guilty suspects don't usually hand themselves in for questioning.'

'The smart ones do. It diverts attention away from themselves.'

'In that case,' said West as she tore a bite out of her pizza, 'he'll have no qualms about talking to us. Once you're off the blower give Duncan a bell, he's still in

Auchinleck. Tell him to take another look around Lea's gaff, a proper look this time.'

'Will do. I'd best organise a warrant too. How will he get in?'

'This is Duncan we're talking about,' said West. 'He'll find a way.'

* * *

Deferring the task of sifting through anything belonging to Rupert Lea, and with it the associated risk of contracting an airborne viral disease, Duncan – hoping to catch a crafty forty winks – parked in a secluded spot beneath the shade of a tree by the railway station and curled up on the back seat, only for his impending catnap to be interrupted by the buzz of his phone.

'Oh, it's you, chief!' he said, suppressing a yawn. 'Are you okay?'

'Aye, not bad,' said Munro. 'In fact, I feel great! And yourself?'

'I'm ready for my pit if I'm honest.'

'Well, can you stay awake a wee bit longer? I need your help.'

'Aye, no bother. Where are you?'

'On my way to the office.'

'Is that wise?' said Duncan. 'I mean, if Westy…'

'Are you not there?'

'No, no. I'm in Auchinleck, on a job.'

'That's even better! You've just saved me at least half an hour. Where will we meet?'

'The car park at the railway station.'

'The railway station?' said Munro. 'Are you on Obs'? Some kind of a stake-out?'

'No, I'm trying to have a wee kip on the back seat.'

'Well, I cannae fault you for that, laddie. I cannae fault you at all.'

* * *

Loitering like a cagey carjacker waiting to deliver the spoils of his latest heist, Duncan, polishing off a packet of peanuts in lieu of his lunch, sat perched on the edge of the bonnet and nodded casually as Munro's ageing Peugeot crept in to view.

'Dear God,' he said as Duncan slipped into the passenger seat. 'I've seen healthier looking folk in the mortuary. Are you okay?'

'Nothing a couple of hours sleep and a double cheeseburger won't cure, chief. You're looking well.'

'I'm on top of the world,' said Munro. 'I'd forgotten just how great it feels to fill your lungs with air and not get out of breath just walking up the street.'

'Good for you. I look forward to feeling like that myself one day.'

'So you're not just here for a nap, are you, laddie? What's the story?'

'Oh, it's our number one suspect in this Nancy Wilson murder,' said Duncan, 'he lives nearby. He disappeared right after her death but now he's back again. Westy's going to give him a grilling while I take a look around his house. Hopefully we'll find something we can use against him. How about you?'

'The same thing,' said Munro, 'only it's this Galbraith fellow I'm after. I have the distinct feeling he's not the paragon of virtue he claims to be.'

'Well you're always on the money with your hunches, chief, but should you be meddling in the case? I mean, no disrespect, but there's your health to consider, and you're retired.'

'I'm as fit as a fiddle and just for the record, DCI Clark in Dumfries requested my assistance personally. Until I can find a link between Galbraith and Flora MacDonald, this will have to do.'

'Okay then, if you're sure. So, what do you need?'

Munro pulled the laptop from the back seat and passed it over.

'I'm not one to impose,' he said, 'you know that, but I cannae find my way around this thing. It's the sums behind the extension at the school I'm after.'

'No problem,' said Duncan. 'I downloaded the FOI for you last night so it's here somewhere. Give me a minute and... okay, so according to this, the quote from Caisteal for the whole project was three hundred and twenty grand.'

'And what did the council actually pay?'

'Three hundred and twenty grand.'

'And the cost to Caisteal? Let me guess...'

'Three hundred and twenty grand.'

'By jiminy, that's a first! Do you not find it funny how the figures tally exactly?'

'Is that not what they're meant to do?'

'Come, come, laddie, this is the real world! You should know by now that when it comes to money and governments no work is ever completed on time or on budget. If anything, Caisteal should have overspent but they didnae. Why? Because if I'm right, they completed the whole job for less than fifty thousand pounds and pocketed the difference.'

'Is that possible?'

'Anything's possible,' said Munro with a smile, 'especially as God blessed Europe with the freedom of movement.'

'You mean cheap labour?'

'I mean cheap everything. If I can prove I'm right, then Galbraith will be going down for a few years at least.'

'How so?'

'Falsifying accounts,' said Munro. 'HMRC are going to love it.'

'Back up a wee bit, chief,' said Duncan. 'If you are right about this then with what they creamed off the budget for themselves, wouldn't Galbraith and Mulqueen be sipping cocktails on the Costa del Sol by now?'

'No,' said Munro. 'If there's one thing about us Scots, laddie, it's the belief that home is where the heart is and that's not some gin palace on the Mediterranean, which is why Galbraith is still teaching at the school. Now, do you remember the other fellow, Jack MacDonald, the postmaster?'

'I do, aye.'

'Do you think you could fetch me details of his bank account? I'll need his wife's too.'

'No bother but as they're both dead it may take a while. Will you not need Galbraith's and Mulqueen's details too?'

'No, no. They're still in the land of the living and it wouldn't do to raise their suspicions, not just yet. Oh, and one more thing, I need to know who the headmaster was before Galbraith.'

'Right you are,' said Duncan, 'but I have to visit our suspect's house first. Do you fancy coming?'

'Aye,' said Munro, 'why not. And after that, I shall head back home. I'm of a mind to have a wee chat with Galbraith before school finishes for the day.'

'Just a word of warning, chief,' said Duncan, 'this fella, Rupert Lea, he and personal hygiene were separated at birth.'

'So you've seen his place already?'

'I have, aye, but it was just a wee peek downstairs.'

'Well, how did you get in if the gentleman in question was AWOL?'

'Uniform used the big key on the back door but it's probably been fixed by now.'

Munro opened the glove compartment and retrieved a small, brown leather pouch.

'Here,' he said, 'you'll be needing these. I've no use for them now.'

'A lock pick set? Jesus, you're a dark horse! Do you know how much trouble I'd be in if I was caught using these?'

'Discretion is the key to avoiding capture,' said Munro. 'Besides, it saves the taxpayer the cost of replacing a window or two. Are you familiar with the tools?'

'Oh, I'm a fast learner, me,' said Duncan. 'Very fast indeed.'

* * *

Believing that every mature adult possessed enough self-esteem to maintain even a rudimentary level of cleanliness, Munro – his lip curling in disgust – reached for his handkerchief as he eyed the empty tins of Spam, soup, Spaghetti Hoops, sweetcorn, sardines, and hot dogs strewn across the kitchen table.

'Dear God,' he said, his nose twitching against the noxious odour, 'it smells like a dog food factory in here.'

'You're not wrong there,' said Duncan, 'still, at least he's getting his five a day.'

'Never in my life have I seen so many bluebottles without a rotting corpse to feast on.'

'Don't be so hasty, chief, we've not looked upstairs yet. Just mind you don't touch anything.'

'Are you familiar with the phrase "sucking eggs"?'

'It's not that,' said Duncan, 'I just don't want you catching Monkeypox, that's all. That could finish you off after what you've been through.'

Aside from a fully-stocked wine rack, a waste paper basket crammed with unopened mail, and two overflowing ashtrays on the floor beneath the window, the lounge was completely empty.

'Dear God,' said Munro as he batted a fly from his forehead, 'the man doesnae have any furniture! Where on earth does he sit?'

'I've a feeling his preferred position is supine,' said Duncan. 'I just hope he's got a half decent bed.'

Munro walked to the corner of the room, squatted by the bin and, using a thumb and forefinger, retrieved a handful of envelopes.

'The man's a millionaire,' he said as he inspected the return addresses, 'because he's not interested in what the bank or the credit card companies have to say.'

'He's not the only one,' said Duncan.

Like the lair of a house-bound hoarder, the main bedroom, with its piles of books, out-of-date magazines, empty wine bottles, crisp packets, two un-ironed shirts hanging from a clothes rail, and a stack of parcels from a well-known internet retailer, was without doubt the perfect environment for a pair of rampant rodents to raise their young.

'Oh Jesus!' said Duncan, daring to drop to his knees. 'He's even got a pot under the bed!'

'You should telephone Charlie, tell her not to go near the chap until he's had a go in the sheep dip.'

'How can folk live like this? Has he no self-respect?'

'Obviously not,' said Munro as he studied the cartons on the bedside table, 'but I wouldnae worry too much, they'll be planting him soon.'

'How so?'

'His medication. This is low dose aspirin, seventy-five milligrams, which means he has a heart condition. And this is Theophylline, which means he's asthmatic too.'

'Asthmatic? And he's smoking like a chimney?'

'That's not all,' said Munro as he waved a third box in the air. 'Metformin. He's a diabetic.'

'He's diabolical,' said Duncan nodding towards a crash helmet sitting on the floor, 'but if the abuse doesn't kill him, the motorbike will.'

Intrigued, Munro picked up the helmet and, tilting it towards the light, scrutinised the strands of hair stuck to the lining and the pair of scuffed, leather gloves tucked inside.

'You do surprise me,' he said, 'I'd have thought a wee action man like yourself would have enjoyed the thrill of two wheels.'

'Not me, chief. I'll leave that to Dougal. He and this Lea fella can talk two strokes to their heart's content. Is something wrong?'

'Leave no stone unturned,' said Munro, 'you should bag this and get it analysed.'

'No need, chief, we've already got Lea's DNA on the database.'

Munro held the helmet aloft and raised his eyebrows.

'Right you are,' said Duncan, 'if you think it will help.'

Dismayed not just by the chaos around him but by the broken table lamp, the torn curtains, and a pair of discarded but perfectly serviceable boots, Munro shook his head and sighed.

'It's not for me to comment on how folk should live their lives,' he said, 'but if there's one thing I cannae abide, it's waste.'

'I'm not with you, chief.'

'Look about you, this place is a temple of neglect. Break something, buy a new one. Call me old-fashioned but I'm of a generation who were raised on the tenet of "make do and mend". We recycled everything long before the Green Party made it the fashionable thing to do.'

'And your point is?'

'This fellow,' said Munro as he pointed out a monitor lying face down on the bed, 'he's obviously a member of the disposable society, I mean, that's no way to treat a television set.'

'Oh, that's not a telly,' said Duncan. 'That's an iMac...'

'I stand corrected.'

'...it's a computer. Let's see what he's been up to, shall we?'

Duncan righted the Mac, hit the power button on the back, and smiled as the screen sprang to life.

'I thought folk these days were more tech-savvy,' he said, 'you know, security conscious. It's not even password protected.'

'Frankly, laddie, I cannae see anyone in their right mind setting foot in this house, let alone touching anything. Not unless they wanted a spell in the ICU.'

'Look at this, chief, he was using it earlier this morning, that must've been before uniform picked him up. At least now we know where he's been the past few days.'

'How so?'

'His search history,' said Duncan. 'See here, he booked a return ticket to Edinburgh online...'

'Edinburgh?'

'Aye, he went to something called "GastroFest" and spent four nights at the Hotel du Vin.'

'It's like I said, the man's a millionaire. Is that you?'

'Almost,' said Duncan, 'I just want a quick look at his recently-viewed files before I bag it up.'

Selecting a folder tagged "NAN", Duncan leaned back and sighed as a multitude of images cascaded down the screen.

'The fella's not right in the head, chief. He's obsessed.'

'Well, there's no question about it,' said Munro, crouching as he squinted at the screen, 'he's a fetish for a certain kind of a lady, that's for sure.'

'You need your glasses, chief, that's not just a certain kind of a lady, they're all the same person. That's Nancy Wilson.'

Intrigued by Lea's fixation and Duncan's apparent complacency, Munro stood up, clasped his hands behind his back and contemplated the ceiling.

'You're not surprised,' he said softly. 'Why is that?'

'Rupert Lea was done for stalking this lassie, chief. A breach of the peace to be precise, but he got an absolute discharge.'

'Did he indeed. Why?'

'Basically because he had a clean sheet.'

'So despite an appearance in court, he continued to hound the poor girl?'

'He did, aye. Let me just display these in chronological before we go, that'll give me an idea of when… oh, this is good! This is very good indeed!'

'Stop havering laddie and tell me what's going on!'

'This picture here,' said Duncan, 'the one of her arriving for work, that was taken the day she died.'

'You're on a roll,' said Munro as he zipped his coat, 'all you have to do now is find the camera.'

'Camera?'

'Well, those photos didnae get onto that computer by themselves now, did they?'

'Oh Christ,' said Duncan glancing around the room, 'that means I've got to rummage through this lot.'

'And you'd be wise to look for anything else that might incriminate the fellow.'

'The camera's plenty for now, chief. I'm not hanging round here any longer than necessary.'

'Well, I hope you've had your jabs,' said Munro. 'I'm away to see Galbraith, I'll telephone you later.'

Chapter 9

Likening his puffy complexion to that of a cabbage patch doll with an underactive thyroid, Dougal, bewildered by the difference between the image on the driving licence and the figure seated before him, smiled at Rupert Lea as West, perturbed by the pungent odour of cannabis and sweat, sniffed the air and opened the window.

'Sorry,' she said, 'it's a bit whiffy in here. I'm Detective Inspector West and this is DS McCrae. Thanks for coming by.'

'No bother,' said Lea, peering through his Coke-bottle glasses, his skinny frame swathed in an over-sized sweater. 'Happy to help.'

'You know this is completely informal, don't you? You've not been accused of anything, so you don't have to answer any questions if you don't want to. We won't hold it against you.'

'And you can leave any time you like,' said Dougal. 'We'll even arrange a lift for you.'

'Smashing,' said Lea. 'So, what do you need to know?'

'Well, at the risk of going over old ground,' said West, 'it's about a young lady you're familiar with, or used to be, anyway. Miss Nancy Wilson.'

'Oh aye, Nancy! She's a beauty, is she not?'

'That is in the eye of the beholder,' said West, 'and going by what I've seen recently, I'm afraid I'd have to disagree.'

'That's probably because you're not that way inclined.'

'Trust me, even if I was, there are some places I just can't go.'

'I'm not with you.'

'She's dead, Mr Lea. I'm sorry to say Miss Wilson was murdered.'

Lea tousled what was left of his straggly, shoulder-length locks, tied them back in a ponytail, and puffed out his cheeks.

'That's a hell of an opener,' he said. 'What was it? A stabbing? Some ned with a blade?'

'We can't go into details,' said Dougal, 'this is an on-going investigation, I'm sure you understand.'

'Aye, of course. Of course. Still, it's a bit of a blow. So, when did this happen?'

'A few days ago,' said West. 'Coincidentally, the same day you disappeared.'

'Oh, so that's why I'm here. Well, just for the record, I didn't disappear, folk are entitled to have a wee break now and then.'

'Quite. Still, you're here now and that's all that matters, so just a few questions, then hopefully we can eliminate you from our inquiry and move on.'

'Easier said than done,' said Lea. 'It's not that easy to move on after a bereavement.'

'You're talking as though you and she were close.'

'No, we weren't. And more's the pity.'

Unnerved by the sly if not sadistic grin that crept across his face, Dougal, desperate to reassert himself, leaned forward and tapped his biro on the desk.

'Let's start at the beginning,' he said firmly. 'Would you mind telling us where you've been?'

'Aye, Edinburgh. *GastroFest*.'

'Which is?'

'The clue's in the title. It's a festival of gastronomy. With a scientific twist.'

'And can you verify that?'

'I can indeed. I've got the train tickets and my hotel reservation.'

'Which hotel?'

'The Hotel du Vin. They'll remember me, I've no doubt about that.'

'Why should they?'

'Because,' said Lea, rubbing the end of his nose, 'they asked me to leave. Some of the other guests had complained about my... it's embarrassing to say.'

'Don't be shy,' said Dougal, 'you're amongst friends here.'

'I have a medical condition. I tend to perspire a lot.'

'That's a bit unfair,' said West, 'but understandable I suppose. Let's talk about Nancy, shall we? You were charged a while back with a breach of the peace, is that right?'

'It is, aye. But I got an absolute discharge.'

'That doesn't necessarily absolve you of any guilt, Mr Lea. Why were you harassing her? It wasn't because you wanted swimming lessons now, was it?'

'Actually, I wouldn't call it harassing,' said Lea. 'More wooing.'

'I see. So you tried to woo her by scaring the living daylights out of the woman? By following her everywhere she went?'

'She didn't respond to my cards or flowers. And she refused to speak to me if I visited her at work.'

'Hardly surprising. So just because she spurned your advances, you thought it was okay to stalk her? Can you not take no for an answer?'

'I thought she was just plain shy,' said Lea, 'you know, a wee wallflower. I thought I might be able to bring her out of her shell.'

'Are you a bit of a fantasist, Mr Lea?' said Dougal. 'I mean, do you play out scenarios in your head of what might have happened between you and Miss Wilson?'

'Oh, that's deep,' said Lea. 'And personal. Deeply personal. I'm afraid I'm not about to share my inner thoughts with the likes of you.'

'Fair enough. So how did you meet?'

'I went to enrol at the leisure centre and she was on the desk.'

West, unable to control herself, chuckled aloud and raised a hand to her mouth in an attempt to stifle her laughter.

'You find that amusing?'

'Sorry,' she said. 'No offence but you don't seem the type.'

'If you must know,' said Lea curtly, 'I was after joining the fitness class. I've let myself go recently. I used to be quite sporty once upon a time.'

'I'm sure you were. So did you join?'

'I did not. No. I got distracted.'

'By Nancy?'

'Aye.'

'And when was the last time you saw her?'

'Oh, a while now. Months, I'd say.'

'So you've not even spoken to her? Or been to her house? I mean, you know where she lives, don't you?'

'Aye, I do,' said Lea, 'but I've kept my distance. You see, Inspector, even though I got off, it was with the caveat that if I ever went near her again, I'd get a custodial.'

'Well, it's nice to see you've been behaving yourself,' said West. 'Tell me, just out of interest, what do you do for a living?'

'Living? You mean work? No, no, I don't work.'

'Is that because you're on benefits? Because of your health?'

'No, it's because I'm frugal and I can live off what I have. I came into some money a while back.'

'Lucky you. And would you care to tell us where this money came from?'

'I would not,' said Lea. 'I'm not being funny, hen, I'm happy to tell you anything you want to know about Nancy, but I'm not here to discuss my personal financial affairs.'

West leaned back, locked eyes with Lea, and pondered for a moment.

'Mind if we take a break?' she said. 'We won't be long.'

'Take as long as you like.'

'Can we get you something? A cup of tea? Coffee maybe?'

'No, you're alright,' said Lea. 'I'm fine just now.'

* * *

West climbed the stairs to the second floor, slumped down on the landing and leaned against the wall, her left foot tapping out an incessant beat like a musician marking time.

'Let me guess,' said Dougal, 'you're not comfortable with the fact that someone who's just pledged his undying love for Nancy Wilson is not showing any remorse.'

'In one,' said West. 'You'd have thought he'd have been mortified, burst into tears even, but nothing, just ho-hum another one bites the dust.'

'Aye, I get that, but do you not think it's because it wasn't much of a shock?'

'You mean like he already knew?'

'Well, it would take the edge off things. Besides, it's not as if she's been the subject of a blackout.'

'No, I suppose not,' said West, sighing as the sound of laboured footsteps echoed down the stairwell. 'The bottom line is we've got nothing on him, so we can't force him to stay.'

'Aye, and the clock's ticking on Nevin too,' said Dougal, 'we should ask The Bear to authorise an extension.'

'Yeah, you're right. Another twelve hours won't hurt; have a word, would you? And you may as well get a car sorted for Lea, let him go but tell him not to go taking any more trips without telling us first.'

* * *

'Are you on the naughty step?' said Duncan, grinning as he plodded down the stairs.

'What are you doing here?'

'I'm away to get some lunch before I keel over, what's your excuse?'

'We're thinking,' said West, 'and it's beginning to hurt.'

'What about?'

'Lea.'

'Is he still here?'

'Yup, but not for long,' said West. 'We're about to let him go.'

'Not so fast,' said Duncan tossing them both a pair of gloves, 'here, you're going to need these.'

Too tired to question his motives, West snapped on the gloves and, waiting for his next move, stared at him despondently.

'Oh cheer up, for Christ's sake,' he said as he pulled a compact digital camera from his pocket.

'Where'd you get that?' said Dougal.

'Lea's place. And I've got his computer too, it's on your desk, you're going to have a ball, trust me.'

'So you've got something?'

'I have indeed,' said Duncan as he passed the camera to West. 'Take a look at that image there…'

'It's Nancy Wilson. Where was this taken?'

'In the office at the leisure centre, miss, but here's the thing, look at the date.'

'I don't believe it,' said West, 'it's the day she died! Duncan, I could kiss you!'

'Cool your jets, miss. I'm spoken for. One more thing, I found a motorcycle helmet and a pair of gloves in the bedroom. I've fast tracked it for analysis.'

'A helmet?' said Dougal. 'I don't recall seeing a bike at his house.'

'It's in the garden, pal, it's hard to spot with all the other junk he's got lying about the place. I've made a note of the index, I'll run it by the DVLA later and make sure it's his.'

'Is that it?' said West.

'Is that not enough?'

'It's plenty. Go get your lunch, you've flipping earned it. Dougal, let's have another word with that lying toad.'

* * *

'Alright?' said West as she sauntered into the interview room. 'Are you sure about that drink?'

'Aye,' said Lea. 'It's kind of you to offer but I'm okay for now.'

'Just as well, because you're going to need a whisky in a minute. Now, just to be absolutely clear, you say the last time you saw Nancy Wilson was months and months ago, is that right?'

Lea smiled and nodded politely.

'Aye, that's right,' he said. 'Months and months ago.'

'Well, the thing is, I'm not sure I believe you. You see, I think you saw her the day she died. I think you were hanging around the leisure centre just like the old days.'

'And what makes you think that?'

'This does,' said West as she laid the camera on the desk.

'I'm not with you,' said Lea. 'What does that have to do with me?'

'We found it in your house…'

'Oh, now hold on!' said Lea. 'You need a warrant before you go nosing round my home!'

'No need to worry on that score,' said Dougal, 'we've got one.'

'...and what's more,' said West, 'this has got lots of lovely pictures of Nancy on it.'

'See here,' said Lea, 'regardless of whether you have a warrant or not, I'm telling you, that's not mine.'

'Well, we'll get it dusted and if we find your prints on it then you'll have some explaining to do. Like how all these photos are on your computer too.'

'You've got my computer?'

'Yup. And that's just for starters.'

Lea rose to his feet, pulled up his jeans, and scowled at West with a smarmy grin smeared across his face.

'Okay,' he said, 'now you've gone too far. I think it's time I left.'

'Sorry,' said West. 'I'm afraid that's not possible anymore.'

'Oh aye? How so?'

'Because I'm arresting you under section 1 of the Criminal Justice Act on suspicion of the murder of Nancy Wilson. You are not obliged to say anything but anything you do say will be noted and may be used in evidence. Do you understand?'

Chapter 10

Set on a quiet country lane surrounded by woodland and wide, open fields, the school in Palnackie – a whitewashed, single-storey building with a moss-laden roof – had, despite the growth of the village, changed little in its two-hundred-year history.

Relishing the warmth of the afternoon sun, Munro, standing with his jacket slung casually over his shoulder, watched as hordes of screaming children fled its granite walls followed at a sedate pace by a colossus of a man with a snowy white beard wearing a jet black suit looking not unlike a Quaker from *Little House on the Prairie*.

'You're not a parent, are you?' said Galbraith as he lumbered across the road.

'Too late for that,' said Munro with a wink. 'It's not changed much, has it?'

'The school? So you're familiar with the place then?'

Munro, guessing Galbraith to be at least ten years his junior, took a deep breath and decided to chance his arm.

'I am,' he said, smiling nostalgically. 'I used to be a pupil here.'

Galbraith shot him a wary glance.

'And when was that?' he asked suspiciously.

'About the time Edison had his light bulb moment. Things were different then of course. Life was better.'

'Put your rose-tinted spectacles away,' said Galbraith, 'things haven't changed that much.'

'Oh, I'm not sure I'd agree with you there,' said Munro as he recalled Duncan's invaluable piece of research. 'The staff didnae have to meet targets in those days, and us weans were allowed to run free. Dinnae get me wrong, we had discipline too, that was thanks to a fellow by the name of Anderson. Eoin Anderson. He ruled the roost with a rod of iron but I'll give him this, he was firm but fair.'

'My philosophy exactly,' said Galbraith, relaxing at the mention of Anderson's name. 'Would you care for a look inside Mr...?'

'Munro. James Munro. Thanks but you're alright. I'd rather keep my memories intact. So, do you teach here then?'

'I'm the headmaster. Galbraith's the name. What brings you here, Mr Munro? I hope you're not ticking things off a bucket list?'

'No, no, I've been meaning to come for some time, but when I heard about Flora MacDonald, well, that just made the trip all the more poignant.'

'Aye, dear Flora. A tragedy for sure. So you knew her?'

'We exchanged pleasantries,' said Munro. 'My late wife, Jean, God rest her soul, and myself would often pop into the post office on our way back from Rascarrel.'

'Rascarrel?'

'Aye, there's some fine walking to be had around the bay. You need a head for heights mind; if the wind's blowing atop the cliff well, you're taking your life in your hands.'

'Oh you're not wrong there,' said Galbraith. 'I know it well. I have one of those fancy holiday homes on the beach, have you seen them? The cabins?'

'No. It's been a while, I'm afraid, and I'm not up to walking much these days.'

'They're something else,' said Galbraith. 'All mod cons, a great view, and we even have a hot tub on the deck.'

'Och, you'll not catch me in one of those, I prefer my creature comforts indoors. So, is that your retirement home then? Feet up by the beach?'

'God no, I'll not be retiring for a while yet, Mr Munro, but I'm good to myself, I'll tell you that. I've invested for the future.'

Munro looked skyward and heaved a sigh.

'I wish I had,' he said. 'You'd think a lifetime in local government would have provided a decent pension, but it doesnae go far. And that was the two of us.'

'So, your wife was in the same line of work?'

'Not quite the same, no,' said Munro. 'She was an admin assistant in the council planning department. Lots of typing and filing, but she liked her boss, a woman called Muldoon.'

'Muldoon?'

'No. Not Muldoon. Mulqueen! That's it, Mulqueen. They got along famously. So she said.'

'I crossed swords with a Mulqueen,' said Galbraith. 'Over the extension at the school.'

'Is that so? Well, who'd have thought, eh? It must be that six degrees of separation you hear folk talk about.'

'Aye, it's a small world, right enough.'

'Did she not want you to build it then? This Mulqueen woman?'

'No, she did not,' said Galbraith. 'Between you and me, Mr Munro, she was that far up her own backside she could see her tonsils. You know the type: doesn't live here, doesn't work here, but thinks she knows best when it comes to the needs of the community.'

'Welcome to the world of democracy,' said Munro. 'Although, she must have wavered, I mean, you got it built after all.'

'We did, aye,' said Galbraith. 'But it came at a price.'

'How so?'

Galbraith, almost tripping over his words, coughed as he cleared his throat.

'I'm speaking metaphorically of course,' he said. 'You know, the stress and the strain of it all, jumping through hoops to get not what we want but what we need.'

'That's them to a T,' said Munro, 'they've not respect for anyone unless they're lining their pockets. I only wish I'd got out sooner and followed a career with a decent pension.'

'You're not the only one, Mr Munro. It's the same for us teachers too but as they say, you can't take it with you so I'm making the most of it now.'

'Good for you.'

'Did you know I've a boat as well? It's nothing grand, mind, but it does the job.'

'A boat?' said Munro. 'Now I'm a wee bit jealous. I used to think I'd be the next Para Handy when I was a wean.'

'Oh I'm not one for sailing, it's too much like hard work. No, if we decide on a trip, I pay someone to skipper the boat for us. We just sit back. And relax.'

'Well, your investments have certainly paid off, Mr Galbraith. A holiday home and a wee boat and you're not even retired. You must be a whizz on the stock market.'

Galbraith glanced at Munro, thought for a moment, then flung his back and laughed.

'The stock market?' he said, smiling as he shook his head. 'That's for gamblers, Mr Munro! See here, the way I see it is, if you're after a good return then it's too risky, and if you play it safe then you'll not get a decent return. If there's one thing I learned from old Jack MacDonald it's that cash is king. There's no doubt about it.'

'Jack MacDonald? Was he not Flora's husband?'

'He was indeed. Husband, friend, confidant, and village postmaster for as long as I can remember; and when it came to figures, he had a mind like a calculator.'

'Have they planted him as well?'

'He went before Flora. Some say it was his passing that finished her off.'

'Dear, dear. So Jack wasnae one for the stocks and shares then?'

'The biggest risk Jack ever took in his entire life was crossing the street. He always said a penny saved was a penny earned and if that didn't work, then if no-one's looking, rob Peter to pay Paul.'

'Wise words,' said Munro. 'You make it sound as though he robbed the entire county.'

Galbraith opened his mouth as if to speak, hesitated for a moment too long, and laughed.

'That would never do,' he said as he brushed the tip of his nose with his finger. 'Well, it's been a pleasure, Mr Munro, but I must get on.'

'Likewise,' said Munro. 'I've not had my lunch so I'm away to the Glenisle for a fish supper. I've not been since my wife passed away.'

'You'll enjoy it,' said Galbraith, 'it's not changed in years.'

* * *

As the first customer of the evening, Munro, having his pick of the tables, ordered his food as he breezed by the bar and sat, much to the bewilderment of the staff, in a small booth with his back to the restaurant where he tucked a napkin into his collar, tipped three spoons of sugar into his tea, and hit redial as he waited for his scampi and chips to arrive.

'Alright, chief?' said Duncan. 'How are you feeling?'

'Never better. And yourself?'

'Shattered, you're not overdoing it, are you?'

'No, no. I'm taking it easy. Are you okay to talk?'

'Aye, all quiet here,' said Duncan. 'Dougal and Westy are still downstairs, I think they're throwing the book at Lea and it's all thanks to you.'

'Me?'

'Aye, you're the one who told me to look for that camera and it's nothing but back to back photos of Nancy Wilson. It may not be enough to nail him just now, but we've time on our side if we need something else.'

'That's not down to me, laddie, you found the images on his computer; you should give yourself a pat on the back.'

'I would if I could reach. So how are things your end? Did you speak with that Galbraith fella?'

'I certainly did,' said Munro, 'and I need another favour.'

'No bother.'

'There's no rush, in your own time.'

'It probably will be.'

'Mulqueen,' said Munro. 'I need to know if she still works for the council or if she's moved on and if she has, then I need an address and anything else you can find.'

'What's brought her out of the woodwork?'

'It seems she wasnae a part of Galbraith's original plan. She muscled her way in.'

'How so?'

'She refused planning permission for the school's extension unless she was recompensed.'

'You mean she was after a backhander?'

'Oh aye,' said Munro. 'And a hefty one at that.'

'Jeez-oh, talk about corruption.'

'I'd rather not, I'm about to have my supper. Did you get anywhere with the MacDonalds' accounts?'

'Not really, chief,' said Duncan. 'I have a copy of Flora's transactions for the twelve months before she died, and she's clean. And I checked Jack MacDonald's history for the twelve months following Caisteal's collapse, and there's nothing there either.'

'As I thought,' said Munro. 'It's cash they would have been dealing with and from what I've heard Jack MacDonald was too clever by half to leave a paper trail.'

'Will I go after Galbraith then?'

'No, you'll not find anything there, but there is something else you can do for me.'

'Just name it.'

'Caisteal. Find out where they held their bank account and when they closed it. It would have been shortly before they rolled the company and the funds would have been taken in cash, not a transfer or a draft.'

'Easy enough,' said Duncan, 'considering the sums involved.'

'And they'd have needed at least two signatories present to make the withdrawal, I want to know who they were.'

'Roger that, chief. Anything else?'

'Aye. The next pint's on me.'

Chapter 11

Torn between tackling the piles of pots, pans, and plates languishing in the sink, checking on Munro, or preparing the report for the procurator fiscal, West, making by far the easiest decision of the day, slumped on the sofa and ordered a takeaway instead, her first sip of red interrupted by the chime of her phone.

'Duncan,' she said, 'nice going today, well done, mate.'

'Thanks very much, miss.'

'To what do I owe the pleasure?'

'Well, I was heading for my pit,' said Duncan, 'but something came up. Are you busy?'

'I've got twenty minutes before my grub arrives...'

'Oh aye? Something healthy no doubt?'

'As always,' said West. 'Prawn toast, spring rolls, spare ribs, Szechuan beef and a special fried rice.'

'You surprise me. No pudding?'

'Chips and curry sauce.'

'You're getting too Scottish for your own good.'

'It's comfort eating.'

'How so?' said Duncan. 'Are you depressed?'

'No, it's Lea,' said West. 'Everything we have is pretty much circumstantial. We still need something concrete, something which incriminates him beyond any doubt.'

'Well, relax, miss. It's your lucky day.'

'Go on then.'

'Okay, but I'm not saying if you're going to get all emotional again.'

'Spit it out.'

'I've just got the results back from FS on the motorcycle gear I sent for testing…'

'And?'

'There were strands of red hair inside the helmet, they're a match for Lea.'

'Well, whoop-de-do,' said West, 'it's his helmet, what do you expect?'

'Wait for it. Gloves.'

'Don't tell me. Sweat stains on the inside. Also a match.'

'Back of the class for being so hasty,' said Duncan. 'They've got Kevlar knuckle protectors stitched beneath the leather.'

'So?'

'Kevlar, miss! It's light, but it's as hard as steel. See here, the inserts are shaped to the fit around the knuckles, which means they're moulded into four small bumps which are blunt and rounded. I've a feeling they'll match the wee dents on Wilson's face.'

'Is that it?' said West. 'You've called me up to tell me you've got a hunch that a scrawny little specimen like Lea punched the hell out of Nancy Wilson?'

'It's not a hunch, miss,' said Duncan. 'It's a fact. DNA taken from blood and tissue samples found on the gloves belongs to Miss Wilson.'

Duncan, imagining the sound of West's jaw hitting the floor, smiled at the ensuing silence.

'Bugger,' said West eventually. 'This means I'll have to cancel my dinner.'

'You will not! There's no point in starving yourself, I mean, it's not as if Lea's going anywhere.'

'You're right, I'll take it with me.'

'With you? Where are you going?'

'Back to the office,' said West as she reached for her coat. 'I'm going to charge Lea.'

'Okey dokey.'

'And look,' said West as she gulped her wine, 'I know you're knackered but can you do me a favour?'

'Aye, why not?' said Duncan. 'I've done plenty of those recently.'

'Call Dougal and tell him to start getting the paperwork in order for the fiscal, I want Lea in court as soon as possible...'

'No problem.'

'...and when you've done that...'

'Are you joking me?'

'...can you nip over to Lea's gaff?'

'Aye okay, if I can get my head down for an hour first.'

'No sweat,' said West. 'Go have a kip, then see if you can raise a SOCO to help you out. Grab anything you can that might be relevant. Anything at all.'

'Roger that, but is what we have not enough?'

'Not quite. We're still missing one important thing.'

'And what would that be?'

'A motive.'

'A motive? Are you joking me? It's the money, is it not?'

West, pondering her own words, returned to the sofa, hung her head, and stared blankly at the floor.

'No,' she said, her voice dropping to a whisper, 'I'm not sure it is.'

'How so?'

'Lea and Wilson weren't an item. They weren't loved-up. So how did he know about it? I mean, she's not exactly going to tell her stalker she's got a stash of cash under the kitchen floor, now, is she?'

'Christ, if you put it like that. Well, what then?'

'Dunno,' said West. 'Maybe he couldn't stand being knocked back. Maybe he couldn't handle a blow to his ego.'

'But you saw her place,' said Duncan. 'You said the perp' was definitely looking for something.'

'I know. And that's what's doing my head in.'

* * *

Oblivious to West hovering in the doorway, Dougal, who preferred to work to the hoot of an owl rather than the roar of the traffic, stood in the gloom of the office with his hands clasped above his head wiggling his hips like a second-rate lap dancer in a working men's club.

'Nice moves,' said West, laughing as she placed a carrier bag on the desk.

'Jeez-oh!' said Dougal as his face flushed. 'What are you doing here?'

'You don't know? The crash helmet? The gloves?'

'Oh that.'

'Oh that!' said West. 'Blimey, don't get too excited. Come on then, what's all the twerking about?'

'I'm celebrating, miss.'

'Don't tell me, you've got a place on *Britain's Got Talent.*'

'Imagine, if you will, the results from forensic services as a cake.'

'A cake?'

'Aye. And I'm just about to ice it.'

'This,' said West, unwrapping the spring rolls, 'I have got to hear.'

'Remember the motorbike outside the leisure centre? The one parked near the front doors?'

'Yeah?'

'I've identified the model. It's an old Yamaha. An XT500.'

'I'll get the champagne.'

'Now, it's only just in frame,' said Dougal, 'the CCTV didn't pan around wide enough to get a view of the whole bike so the problem we have is, even if Duncan gets the DVLA to confirm that the bike in Lea's back yard belongs to him, it doesn't prove that it's the one outside the centre...'

'And that's a reason to celebrate?'

'...unless it has two distinctive scratches on the left-hand side of the petrol tank and a cracked wing mirror.'

'Well, you know what to do.'

'I do indeed. I was about to scoot over there now and take a few pictures.'

'What with?' said West. 'Infrared? Get a grip Dougal, get it brought over and have SOCOs go over it, right now I need you to get that report ready for the fiscal. I want it on her desk first thing in the morning.'

'Aye okay, but can I go fetch some food first?'

'No need. I've got a Chinese banquet for two if you fancy it.'

'Smashing. I'll stick the kettle on. Where is Duncan anyway?'

'Where all sane people should be. In bed. He's having a nap before heading over to Lea's place to bag up everything he can.'

'Oh we're almost there!' said Dougal. 'I can feel it in my bones.'

'Don't count your chickens,' said West, 'we've still got a couple of hurdles to jump. Right, let's eat before I dive downstairs to charge Lea and oh, before you get stuck into that report, do me a favour and tell Nevin he's free to go, will you? There's no point in holding the poor sod any longer, put him out of his misery.'

* * *

Although the shiny, blue, waterproof mattress on which he dozed was infinitely more comfortable than the grubby, worn version lying on his bedroom floor, Nevin, due to the dipping temperature and unbearable silence, was unable to relax.

Startled by the sound of the door, he sat up, shielded his eyes from the harsh overhead light, and squinted at the figure in the doorway.

'It's not morning already, is it?' he said.

'No, no,' said Dougal. 'It's just the back of midnight.'

'Oh that's smashing, that is. So why have you woken me? Did you bring my clothes? It's Baltic in here.'

'I'm afraid not,' said Dougal. 'You can wait for them if you like, or we can send them on.'

'Send them on? Where to?'

'Your house of course.'

'I'm not with you,' said Nevin. 'Why send them there?'

'Because you're free to go.'

'Just like that?'

'Aye.'

'No explanation? No apology?'

'Well, you're not guilty,' said Dougal, 'so there's your explanation. And sorry for detaining you. There's your apology. Cheery-bye.'

Chapter 12

Confident that the only person likely to approach him at two o'clock in the morning would be a ne'er-do-well offering his services as a fence for stolen property, Duncan bounded to the rear of the house, picked the lock with the dexterity of a safe-breaker and, as a safeguard against contaminating himself rather than the evidence, donned a Tyvek suit before heading to the bedroom.

Aware that the focused beam of a flashlight bouncing off the walls was a sure-fire way of drawing attention to himself, he flicked on the main light, gazed despondently around the room and, unable to distinguish between items which were soiled and those that were clean, picked his way through the piles of laundry scattered about the place until, conspicuous by its delicate fragrance, he fished a ladies' cashmere scarf from beneath a sweat-stained pillow.

Flinching at the thought of Lea's sordid fixation, he bagged it up and turned his attention to the first of five battered cardboard boxes – which was filled, unsurprisingly, with empty wine bottles – before grinning excitedly as he pulled from the second, nestling beneath a tarnished roasting dish, several cassette tapes, an old calendar featuring the scantily clad cast members of

"Baywatch", a thermal balaclava, a pair of waterproof leggings, and a black anorak.

Dismissing the rest of Lea's possessions as worthless bric-a-brac not even worthy of a charity shop donation, he made his way downstairs and stopped as an inexplicable urge, brought about by a strip of silver gaffer tape at the foot of the mattress, forced him to return to the bedroom.

Assuming it to be nothing more than a typically Lea-esque method of repair, he squatted down, tossed the crumb-laden sheet to one side and, half expecting to unleash a nest of beasties from their hiding place, tentatively peeled it back before dashing downstairs to fetch another bag.

* * *

'Duncan,' said West, hollering down the phone. 'How are you getting on?'

'Result, miss. In fact, it's like winning a jackpot on the puggie,' he replied as he flung the final sack into the boot of his car.

'The what?'

'The puggie. It's a fruit machine.'

'Yeah, of course it is. Well, don't keep it to yourself, come on.'

'Hold on,' said Duncan as he buckled up and locked the doors. 'Okay, first of all I found some more biker gear; some waterproofs and, get this, a black anorak.'

'Blinding! Is it the same one the bloke on the CCTV's wearing?'

'It's an anorak, miss. And it's black. That's all I know.'

'Sorry, so go on. What else?'

'A ladies' scarf and it reeks of perfume.'

'You're sure?' said West. 'I mean you're sure it's a ladies' scarf and it's perfume, not aftershave?'

'I think I've been around long enough to tell the difference.'

'Alright, keep your hair on! God, you're tetchy when you're tired! Is that it?'

'No, no,' said Duncan. 'You know how it works, always save the best for last.'

'Knock me out.'

'Nine thousand, two hundred, and eighty quid.'

'You what?'

'All in used twenties.'

'Holy cow, so that's the money he's been living off.'

'Obviously,' said Duncan, 'and needless to say it's not the fruits of honest labour either, although I have to say I thought he'd have been a bit more imaginative when it came to hiding it. I mean, in the mattress, for God's sake.'

'You are kidding? He's a bleeding comedy character, he really is. Okay, give that lot to the SOCO, he can take it for analysis while you…'

'No can do, miss. I'm on my lonesome. No SOCOs available until the morning and no disrespect but I'm not driving all the way to Glasgow to hand this to FS, not just now anyway.'

'No,' said West, 'that would be too much to ask.'

'Indeed it would. And yourself? What's happening there?'

'I've charged Lea but he's still protesting his innocence.'

'What did you expect him to do?'

'I was hoping he'd crumble but, heigh-ho, with any luck he'll be in court by lunchtime. Right, have you finished there now?'

'Aye, all done, why? Don't tell me you're needing another favour?'

'Not me,' said West. 'Dougal does. Can you get to that motorbike in Lea's garden?'

'Not without a machete but I can try. Why?'

'Dougal reckons it might be the same one that's on the CCTV.'

'How will we know?'

'Two big scratches on the petrol tank and a broken mirror.'

'And if it is, does that mean we have him hook, line, and sinker?'

'Maybe,' said West. 'Maybe.'

* * *

To a rank outsider, the characters in the office – West staring blankly into space as she wrangled with thoughts of the real motive behind Lea's actions, Duncan flopped over the desk with his head on his arms trying to catch up on his sleep, and Dougal lethargically assigning his Focus Magic software the relatively simple task of matching two disparate images – looked not unlike a bunch of defeated poker players after an all-night session of five card stud.

Unaware of the effect that his unbridled enthusiasm might have on his unsuspecting colleagues, Dougal, the only one whose brain was still functioning on something approaching full capacity, leapt to his feet with a triumphant yell.

'You beauty!' he said as Duncan all but fell from his seat.

'What is it with you! Are you trying to give me a heart attack?'

'He's got a point,' said West looking like a startled bunny. 'Couldn't you keep it down a bit?'

'Well, pardon me for sealing his fate,' said Dougal indignantly. 'I'm only doing my job.'

'Go on then, let's have it.'

'The motorbike at the leisure centre. It's Lea's.'

'And you tried to put me in my coffin for that? Christ, what time's the café open?' said Duncan. 'I'm famished.'

'Anytime now.'

'I'll go,' said West. 'I could do with the walk.'

'No need.'

Unsure whether to follow her instinct and react with joy or erupt in a fit of impulsive fury, West unfortunately chose the latter.

'What the bleeding hell are you doing here?'

'Nice to see you too, Charlie,' said Munro with a smile. 'I bring you breakfast and joy. There's enough for everyone.'

'You're meant to be resting! Why aren't you on Islay?'

'Boredom, Charlie. And you know what they say about the devil and idle hands.'

'I could swing for you! Have you any idea how worried we've been? You're meant to be getting better and here you are jeopardising your health! No, hold on, more to the point, have you any idea how much I paid for that flipping cottage just because I wanted you to…?'

'Now, now, now!' boomed DCI Elliot as he blundered through the door, 'what's all the racket about?'

'Uh-oh,' said Duncan, 'that's my cue to leave, I'm not getting in the way of The Bear.'

Elliot turned to Munro and raised his arms.

'James! By God, it's good to see you!' he said. 'How have you been?'

'Aye, okay,' said Munro. 'I'm still breathing, so that's a bonus.'

'Let's have a chat before you go," Elliot said. "Charlie, a wee word if I may.'

* * *

West, likening the walk along the corridor to a sprint along the green mile, followed Elliot sheepishly to his office and closed the door.

'Have a seat.'

'No, I'm alright thanks.'

'As you wish,' said Elliot. 'No need to look so scared, Charlie, I've not brought you here for a reprimand.'

'That's a relief.'

'Listen, I know how you feel and how upset you are about James.'

'Really?' said West sarcastically. 'Sorry, sir, but I'm not sure you do.'

'Well, how's this for starters: you and he have a bond. He pulled you out of the mire and for that, you're grateful, so much so that you worry about him; after all, he's been like a father to you and you lost your temper because you don't want to see him planted before his time. And you worry because you think he's not looking after himself.'

'Alright,' said West. 'You win.'

'The thing is, Charlie, it's a two-way street. James has nothing but the utmost respect and admiration for you, but he's not one for showing his feelings, especially since Jean passed away.'

'Only natural, I suppose.'

'You probably thought he felt fine about having that operation,' said Elliot, 'you probably thought, oh, it's the same old James, tough as old boots, nothing to worry about, *"och it's fine I'll be out in a jiff"*. The fact of the matter is, he didn't think he was coming out, Charlie. He even made a will.'

'You are joking?' said West.

'I kid you not. Of course, I'm not at liberty to divulge the details of the will,' said Elliot, 'even though I witnessed it myself, but I will tell you this: if he wasn't here right now, you'd have a roof over your head and you'd not have to worry about earning a living anymore. Do you get what I'm saying?'

'Thanks,' said West. 'That makes me feel a whole lot better.'

'My pleasure. Now go easy on him. He may be getting on in years but I'll tell you this for nothing – he could still run rings around the likes of you.'

* * *

West, feeling like an eight year old who'd been chastised for being selfish rather than an adult who'd failed to keep her emotions in check, returned to her desk and smiled at the sight of Munro wiring into a bacon roll, thankful, despite the risk to his health, that a semblance of normality had returned to the office.

'My fault,' she said, 'I was out of order. I just don't want you knocking on heaven's door, that's all.'

'Och, dinnae go all Bob Dylan on me,' said Munro, 'I cannae stand sentimentality.'

'All the same, a little bit of courtesy wouldn't go amiss, Jimbo. You could've said you were coming back instead of ignoring my calls. Believe it or not, there are some people who care about you.'

'Point taken, lassie. Point taken. So, you lot look as though you've been binging on box sets. What's the story?'

Dougal grabbed his laptop and sat next to Munro while West, hoping some third-party input might alleviate her anxiety, sat on the edge of the desk and filched a fried egg sandwich from the bag.

'Have you lot kissed and made up?' said Duncan as he poked his head around the door. 'Only there's a call I need to make.'

'Go ahead,' said West, 'it's all sweetness and light in here.'

'I must be in the wrong place then. You okay, chief?'

'Never better,' said Munro. 'So, who's going first?'

'I will,' said Dougal. 'Do you want the full story, boss, or the abridged version?'

'Stick to the salient points, laddie. I may expire at any moment.'

'Right you are. So, in a nutshell, Nancy Wilson, a thirty-something office worker and swimming instructor, was bludgeoned to death at the leisure centre in Auchinleck.'

'And what do we know about her?'

'Not much, boss. Apart from her address and her age and the fact that she voted SNP in the last election, there's pretty much nothing on her.'

'Nothing on her?' said Munro. 'She didnae drop from the sky, laddie! She must have some kind of a history. Did you not check with her pals at work?'

'I did, but the best they could do was to tell me she was a vegetarian and drank organic white wine.'

Munro gave Dougal a sideways glance, huffed, and shook his head.

'You surprise me, laddie. It's not like you to have your head in the clouds.'

'Sorry?'

'This Wilson girl! At some point in the past she'd have applied for the role of instructor at the leisure centre, am I right?'

'Aye, I imagine so.'

'Then someone must have interviewed her to assess her suitability for the job?'

'Okay.'

'Ergo, someone must have her CV! And what would her CV contain? Her name, her address, a date of birth, previous employers, education, marital status, shall I go on?'

'No,' said Dougal forlornly, 'you're alright.'

'And what about social media? Is she not on that snappy-chat, or linked-up, or grinder?'

Duncan, unable to contain himself, raised his head and howled with laughter as West tried desperately not to choke on her egg sandwich.

'Was it something I said?' said a bemused Munro.

'Don't worry, Jimbo,' said West, 'we've checked social media and she's not on any of it, especially not Grindr.'

'Then we'd best move on before I give you cause for more hilarity. Dougal, suspects?'

'We had two in the frame, boss. The first fella went on a couple of dates with Wilson and matched a figure caught on CCTV outside the leisure centre on the day that she died, but after questioning, and in the light of new evidence pertaining to the second suspect, he was released without charge. The second suspect, one Rupert Lea, has been charged. He was arrested under Section 38 a few years back for stalking her but got an absolute discharge. He claims he's innocent but every shred of evidence we have says otherwise.'

'And what evidence is that?' said Munro. 'Is it enough to incriminate the fellow?'

'Undoubtedly, boss.'

'Then what's the problem?'

'The problem,' said West, 'is the motive. You see, Jimbo, it all points to the perp' going after a substantial amount of cash Wilson had hidden in her house, and the only way to access that cash was to find a locket she owned which contained a code.'

'You're losing me, lassie.'

'Sorry. The locket contained a pin number which opened a safe, and that's where she kept the cash.'

'But they didn't find it? The locket?'

'No, she was wearing it under her top, but bearing in mind she and Lea hardly even spoke, how did he know to look for a locket? How did he know it contained a PIN number? How did he know it would open a safe? And more to the point, how did he know about the cash in the first place?'

'Dear, dear, dear, I see your dilemma,' said Munro. 'So tell me, Charlie, what does your gut say?'

'It says get some Imodium.'

Munro smiled and popped the lid on his takeaway tea.

'Tell me about the evidence against this Lea fellow,' he said. 'What exactly do you have?'

'For starters,' said Dougal, 'we have Lea's computer which contains dozens and dozens of photos of Nancy Wilson, the most recent of which was taken not just on the day that she died but actually inside her office. Lea also owns a motorbike which was captured on CCTV outside the leisure centre.'

'And have you a weapon?' said Munro. 'Because you'll not get far without one.'

'We have,' said Dougal. 'A pair of reinforced motorcycle gloves belonging to Lea. They went for analysis and came back with blood and tissue fragments on the knuckles, both of which matched positive for Nancy Wilson which proves beyond any doubt that they were worn during the attack.'

Munro sat back with a jolt.

'Are you saying he punched her to death?'

'Yes, and that's just it!' said West. 'That doesn't add up either!'

'Why not?'

'Well, apart from the fact that there's no way he could have known about the money, he's a scrawny runt! A lightweight! He couldn't punch his way out of a paper bag.'

Dougal turned the laptop to face Munro and slid it across the desk.

'Here you go, boss. As you can see, he looks like a stalker, I'll give him that, but a murderer?'

Munro took his spectacles from his pocket, studied the image on the screen, and walked to the back of the room with his hands clasped firmly behind his back.

'The fellow on the screen,' he said, 'does he have any previous? Anything on record?'

'No,' said Dougal, 'just the Section 38 we told you about.'

'And there's nothing before that?'

'Not a sausage.'

'So you cannae actually prove he is who he says he is?'

'I'm not with you, boss.'

'Oh come on,' said Munro, 'you know how it works, laddie. You arrest a man, he gives you his name. You charge him, you take his prints and his DNA, and you assign one to the other. But what if he's not given you his real name?'

'Well, we check,' said Dougal, 'records, registers…'

'But he could have been living under an assumed name for years and if he's not been in trouble before you're none the wiser! To coin a phrase, you're humped! Unless of course, serendipity comes knocking at the door.'

'Don't tell me,' said West, 'she's outside right now.'

'She is indeed.'

'And pray, where exactly are you going with all this?'

Munro turned to West and smiled softly.

'I'll tell you where I'm going, Charlie,' he said with a wink. 'The gentleman on that screen is not who you think it is. It's a chap called Craig McPherson.'

'I knew it,' said West, 'it's always the mind to go first. Just what the hell are you talking about?'

'I've just told you lassie, that gentleman is Craig McPherson. I'd stake my life on it. What's left of it anyway.'

'How can you be so sure?'

'I'll be brief,' said Munro. 'Several years ago, a woman by the name of Flora MacDonald vanished from her home in Palnackie. This week she turned up again. Her body was found stuffed up a chimney.'

'Blimey,' said West. 'Interesting, but what's that got to do with the price of eggs?'

'A local lad also went missing, coincidentally the night before Mrs MacDonald disappeared off the face of the earth. That lad was Craig McPherson. An amateur boxer no less.'

'Good story,' said West, 'but there's probably tons of red-haired boxers about the place. What makes you so sure it's him?'

'His eyes,' said Munro. 'He took a hammering in the ring which left him with one eye watching the sunset while the other was waiting for the sunrise.'

'There's one way to find out,' said Dougal, 'the National Records of Scotland, I'll take a wee look now.'

West stood up, ruffled her hair, and stared at Munro.

'Sometimes,' she said playfully, 'there are moments when I wish I'd never met you. Alright, even if we assume what you say is true and he's been living under a false name for the last few years, there's still one thing I just don't buy.'

'And what's that?'

'That Lea has the ability to pummel anyone. Have you seen him? He's like a stick insect with a beer belly.'

'You'd be surprised,' said Munro. 'Trust me, Charlie, even the bad boxers know how to land a punch, even those that havenae been in the ring for years.'

'Okay. Then the first thing I need to do is prove that they're both the same bloke. Was he done for anything when he was living as McPherson?'

'Now now, Charlie, you're letting yourself down,' said Munro. 'If he had, do you not think his DNA would have come up on a cross-match?'

'So he wasn't convicted of anything?'

'Not a dickie bird,' said Munro. 'He was cautioned a few times for causing a disturbance but that was as bad as it got.'

'Bugger.'

'Mind you, you could always run his prints through the system, they'll be there.'

'Of course!'

'Or if you're in a hurry, why not nip downstairs and simply ask him yourself?'

'No need!' said Dougal excitedly, 'I've got him here! Craig McPherson changed his name by deed poll six years ago!'

* * *

Duncan, groaning with despair, cursed as he slammed his phone on the desk and buried his head in his hands.

'Are you okay?' said West. 'Number engaged?'

Duncan slowly raised his head.

'Has that report gone to the fiscal yet?'

'Not yet,' said Dougal. 'It's still too early.'

'Well, hang fire, there's something you need to know.'

West, concerned by his pained expression, leaned on the desk and stared him in the eye.

'What's up?' she said. 'It's not a dodgy bacon roll, is it?'

'I wish it was,' said Duncan. 'That was the DVLA. They've confirmed Rupert Lea as the keeper of the motorbike.'

'Well, that's great isn't it? I mean, that's just what we want!'

'Aye, but the thing is, Lea doesn't have the official paperwork yet and that's because the DVLA are amending the log book. They're registering a change of ownership.'

'I'm not sure I like the sound of this.'

'He's not had it long,' said Duncan. 'He bought it off a fella called John Nevin.'

Munro, surprised to see the normally docile Dougal twitching with anger, sat back to enjoy what would undoubtedly be a lacklustre bout between a couple of mismatched middleweights.

'That doesn't get Lea off the hook!' said Dougal stabbing the air with his finger. 'He could've been riding that bike for weeks while the DVLA amend the details!'

'Aye, right enough,' said Duncan lethargically, 'he could've been, but he's not insured.'

'Well, that's not unusual around here! Besides, he's got all the bike gear in his house!'

'I'm not a dafty, I found the stuff, remember? The question is: how long has he actually had the bike?'

'Obviously long enough to scoot down the centre and batter Miss Wilson to death!'

'We don't know that for sure,' said Duncan, 'I mean we've only just found it ourselves.'

'The log book! Call the DVLA again, he has to enter the date that he purchased the bike on the log book!'

'I'll not dispute that,' said Duncan, 'but he doesn't have to enter the right date, does he?'

Scoring the bout as a win on points in Duncan's favour, Munro turned his attention to West and, watching as she paced the floor in frustration, waited for the penny to drop.

'I've got it!' she said, clicking her fingers. 'Jimbo, this McPherson geezer, if he was a boxer then he must've trained somewhere, right?'

'Aye, of course he did.'

'Then maybe there's a connection there. Maybe that's where he and Nevin met each other.'

'Hallelujah,' said Munro. 'It was a long time coming but it was worth the wait.'

'I don't suppose you know where he trained, do you?'

'As a matter of fact,' said Munro as he flicked through his notebook, 'I do. The Doonhamers boxing club on Irving Street.'

'Irving Street? Where's that?'

'Dumfries.'

'Right, Duncan can you…?'

'Are you joking me?'

'Oh come on,' said West, 'you look the part! I can't very well send Dougal now, can I? No offence, mate.'

'Blues and twos,' said Munro. 'You could be there in an hour.'

'Aye, go on then,' said Duncan. 'But I'm having the weekend off.'

'Good man. Just say you're trying to trace an old mate or something, you know the score, and give me a bell as soon as you're done. Dougal, get Nevin picked up as soon as possible, please. I'm going to introduce Jimbo to Rupert Lea.'

Chapter 13

Too polite to mention anything, Munro, unsettled by the pervasive pong hanging in the air, pulled a handkerchief from his pocket, delicately dabbed the tip of his nose and, by a process of elimination, identified Lea as the source of the noxious odour.

'You alright?' said West, covering her mouth as she uttered a gentle cough. 'Can we get you anything?'

'Not unless you have a sauvignon on the go,' said Lea.

'Maybe next time. For the benefit of the tape, I am DI West, also present is James Munro. Would you state your name, please?'

'Again?'

West stared at Lea and raised her eyebrows.

'Rupert Lea.'

'You're sure about that?'

'Come again?'

'Never mind,' said West. 'So, down to business.'

'Business? I thought we were done. I thought you were shipping me off to court.'

'We are. In a bit. Just a few more questions to get through first.'

Lea leaned back, wiped his mouth with the back of his hand, and squinted at Munro through his pebble glasses.

'Who are you?' he said. 'Some kind of a lawyer?'

'I'm a kind of something,' said Munro. 'But not a lawyer, no.'

'No, you don't look the type,' said Lea. 'I know, you're one of those psychoanalyst fellas who sit there saying nothing, just scribbling wee notes on that pad of yours.'

'As you can see,' said Munro, smiling at his choice of words, 'I have neither a pad nor a pen, but I do have a few questions.'

'Well, on you go.'

'All in good time. As I'm sure you know, it's good manners to let the ladies go first.'

'I never had you down as a biker, Mr Lea,' said West. 'How long have you been riding?'

'I've not ridden for a while.'

'Is that because of your eyesight?'

'No. I've a different pair for distance.'

'I'm glad to hear it,' said West. 'Tell me, if you've not ridden for a while then why is there a motorcycle in your garden?'

'I'm getting on the road again. I had an urge.'

'Did you indeed? And is this urge the result of some mid-life crisis?'

'Not at my age,' said Lea. 'I don't drive and I need transport, it's as simple as that.'

'Fair enough. Where'd you get it?'

'I bought it. Legit. Three hundred quid.'

'Sounds like a bargain,' said West. 'And did you get it from a dealer or was it a private sale?'

'I got it off a pal.'

'And does your pal have a name?'

'He does,' said Lea, 'but I'm not giving it to you.'

'And why's that?'

'Because I'm not letting you put him through the same kind of hell I've had to endure.'

'Oh come on,' said West, grinning, 'it's not been that bad, has it?'

'Is there a point to this?'

West stood up, tucked her chair beneath the desk, and leaned against the wall.

'Did you collect the bike yourself?' she said, slipping her hands into her pockets. 'Or did your mate drop it off?'

'He dropped it off,' said Lea. 'I'm not legal on it yet.'

'And when was that?'

'A few days ago, who knows, I'm not one for keeping track of time.'

'No, I imagine the days just seem to blend into one continuous blur for you. Did he drop anything else off when he delivered the bike?'

'He did, aye,' said Lea. 'A manual, a plug spanner, some oil, and a foot pump.'

'And did he leave them in the garden too?'

'No, in the house.'

West glanced at Munro, raised the corner of her mouth, and returned to her seat.

'Inside the house?'

'Aye, on the floor. In the living room.'

'And what about the helmet?'

'I don't have a helmet,' said Lea. 'I've not bought one yet.'

'Then how do you explain the one we found in your bedroom?'

'I can't help you there. I told you, I don't have one.'

'Like you don't have a camera?'

'Aye, like I don't have camera.'

'Have you any idea what you do have in your bedroom?'

'Not really, no. I should have a clear out but you know how it is.'

'Quite. So, your mate,' said West, 'you say he left you a manual and some other stuff; how did he get into your house?'

'Keys of course. I gave him a set of keys and he let himself in.'

'Is that because you knew you'd be away?'

'No,' said Lea, 'to be honest I could've been in my pit when he came. Or down the shops. Or in the bathroom.'

'And what happened to the keys?'

'He pushed them back through the letterbox, I found them on the... oh, hold a minute, you say you found a helmet in my bedroom? Well, that explains it, he must've dropped that off too.'

'That's what I thought.'

'Nice one,' said Lea. 'That's saved me a few quid.'

'Will you excuse us for a moment?' said West. 'We won't be long. Interview suspended. DI West and Mr Munro are leaving the room.'

* * *

West strode purposefully to the end of the hallway and, despite the fact that they were well out of earshot, spoke as if plotting a coup in the corridors of power.

'Well?' she said, lowering her voice. 'What do you think?'

'You have to remember I've not been involved in this case, Charlie, but if you're asking for a character assessment then, for what it's worth, I'm inclined to believe the fellow.'

'So am I,' said West.

'Especially having seen his place, it really is...'

'Hold on!' said West. 'What do you mean, you've seen his place?'

Munro, staggered that he of all people should be caught out by a simple slip of the tongue, smiled gently and cleared his throat.

'I've a confession to make,' he said. 'I was with Duncan when he found the computer in Lea's bedroom.'

'You've got some explaining to do!'

'Aye, but now is not the time nor the place. So, what do you think?'

'I think our mate Lea's been set up and I think I know who by.'

'And is that based on fact, Charlie, or is that your gut instinct?'

'One hundred percent instinct, Jimbo. The problem now is, I've got to prove it.'

* * *

West, savouring the lengthy but nonetheless enjoyable silence, gently tapped the voice recorder as Munro, head bowed as if lost in thought, walked the perimeter of the interview room at a painfully slow pace before coming to a halt directly behind Lea's chair.

'Tell me, Craig,' he said, 'do you not miss Palnackie?'

'Palnackie? God no, it's a bit too quiet for my...'

Saying nothing Munro returned to the desk at the same leisurely pace, eased himself into his chair and, after much deliberation over which one to choose, looked McPherson in the eye.

'Let's talk about Flora MacDonald,' he said.

'Who?'

'Come, come, you've had a good run for your money, it's time to come clean, son, the game's a bogey.'

McPherson swallowed hard, shrugged his shoulders, and smiled contemptuously.

'You've lost me,' he said. 'I've really no idea who...'

'See here,' said Munro, 'I'm not a patient man, Mr McPherson, so here's the deal: we have enough evidence stacked against you to put you away for the murder of Nancy Wilson.'

'Oh how many times? I've told you, I didn't do it!'

'I believe you.'

'What?'

'I believe you. And DI West believes you too. But a jury willnae, not when they see the evidence. However,

126

strange as it may seem, you still have a choice. You still have a chance to get yourself off the hook.'

'How so?'

'See here,' said Munro. 'If you go down for the murder of Nancy Wilson then it'll be at least thirty years before you're even eligible for parole. But let's be honest with ourselves, with your track record you simply dinnae have it in you to batter a piece of haddock let alone a defenceless wee lassie.'

'That's what I've been trying to say.'

'Which leads me to believe that if you were in some way responsible for the death of Flora MacDonald, then it would have been accidental, which would result in the lesser charge of manslaughter. So, what's it to be?'

McPherson sat perfectly still, took a deep breath, then looked to the ceiling and sighed.

'How long?' he said. 'How long would I get for manslaughter?'

'That would depend on the motive and the circumstances.'

'Well what if... what if hypothetically speaking, I didn't actually kill her. Not even accidentally. What if she'd died of natural causes and I just happened to be there when it happened?'

'Well, if you've a decent brief,' said Munro, 'then it seems to me the worst you could be tried for is failing to report a death, unless of course there's more to it than that.'

'But either way, the sentence, it'll not be long?'

'Not by comparison. No.'

Though hardened to some of the most stomach-churning sights any serving officer might expect to see, West couldn't help but shudder as McPherson loosened his ponytail and unleashed a torrent of dandruff into the air.

'Okay,' he said. 'There's a fella in Palnackie, the headmaster at the school, his name's Galbraith. I used to do some work for him.'

'What sort of work?' said West.

'Odd jobs mainly. Just fixing things up. He knew I was strapped for cash and that I'd do anything for a few quid.'

'Go on.'

'He gave me a job. He said Jack MacDonald...'

'The postmaster?' said Munro.

'Aye, Jack MacDonald the postmaster. He said he had a serious amount of cash hidden about his house that was rightfully his. He said he'd give me five hundred quid if I could find it.'

'So you took him up on his offer?'

'Aye of course, I'd have been silly not to. I figured it must have had something to do with Jack's fiddling.'

'Fiddling?'

'There were rumours,' said McPherson, 'no-one knew for sure but folk were saying Jack was in the habit of claiming pensions for folk who'd been dead for years.'

'And had he?'

'I doubt it,' said McPherson. 'He was as straight as they come.'

'So, back to the money. What happened?'

'Well, I figured it was a no-brainer. I mean, Jack himself had been planted the year before so it was only Mrs MacDonald in the house. I waited for her to go out and nipped in for a wee look around, only she hadn't gone out at all.'

'And she caught you?' said West.

'She did, aye. She looked... not so much scared, more surprised. I mean, we knew each other, right? So I says to her just relax, tell me where the money is and I'll be off.'

'And did she?'

'Aye, just like that. But then I thought; what if she goes to the police? I'd have no chance, so I told to keep her quiet.'

'So you threatened her?' said Munro. 'You threatened an old lady?'

'No, no,' said McPherson. 'Not really threatened, just asked her, told her to keep her mouth shut. That's when she collapsed. She just lay there with her mouth open, not moving.'

'And you panicked?'

'What do you think?' said McPherson. 'Of course I panicked! I went home, fetched my tools, went back to the house and I wrapped her in a sheet. Then I realised I couldn't bury her, the garden's all paved over and I didn't have time to dig it up, not at that time of night.'

'So you pushed her up the chimney?'

'I know it sounds bad but here was nowhere else for her to go! I took some bricks from the back of the chimney, sealed it up and gave it a lick of paint. I'm not proud of it. I did say a prayer before I left.'

'I'm sure that made all the difference,' said West. 'So, what did you do with the money? Did you keep it for yourself?'

'I'm not that stupid. If Galbraith found out I'd legged it with his money he'd have stuck me up the chimney with her. No, no, I took the cash straight round to his place.'

'And that was it?'

'No,' said McPherson, 'not by a long chalk. He took the money, gave me my five hundred quid and told me to wait. About a half an hour later, he comes back struggling with this wee safe and an envelope, then he gave me an address and told me to take it there. He said I was to make sure the safe was well hidden.'

'And you took it Miss Wilson's house,' said Munro. 'In Auchinleck?'

'I did, aye.'

'And was she expecting it?'

'No. She got the fright of her life when I showed up…'

'Hardly surprising.'

'…but after I'd given her the envelope she calmed down and left me to it.'

'Do you know what was in the envelope?' said West.

'Well, I assume it was a letter,' said McPherson, 'and there was something else, something small and hard, like a coin maybe.'

'And that's it?'

'Pretty much, aye.'

'It's not though, is it?' said West. 'What about the eleven grand you've got hidden in your mattress?'

McPherson, looking more than a little startled, stared at West, shook his head, and laughed.

'Eleven grand?' he said.

'Don't tell me,' said West, 'let me guess. You haven't got eleven grand, have you?'

'Oh but I have,' said McPherson. 'Sorry, I'm just surprised, that's all. I've got to hand it to you, you lot are good at your job. Very good indeed.'

'Thanks very much. Maybe you can mention that next time you're on TripAdvisor.'

'Look, I figured I couldn't stay in Palnackie, okay? I thought as soon as word got out that Mrs MacDonald was missing then folk would start asking questions, the police would come, and I'd be for it, so I went back to Galbraith.'

'What for?'

'I thought I'd chance my arm,' said McPherson, 'I mean, five hundred quid's not going pay the rent for long, is it? I figured I had nothing to lose so I says to him if he wants me to keep quiet then it's going to cost him.'

'So Galbraith gave you eleven thousand pounds,' said Munro, 'is that right?'

'No, no,' said McPherson. 'He gave me twenty. And he bought the house in Auchinleck, on condition, mind, that I never returned to Palnackie. Not unless I wanted a dip in the harbour.'

'And ever since then you've been living as Rupert Lea?'

'Aye, right enough.'

'And does Galbraith know of your pseudonym?'

'Christ, no! And he'd better not find out, not now.'

'Rest assured,' said Munro, 'your secret's safe with us but I'm afraid I cannae guarantee it will remain a secret once the courts and the press get to hear of it. All I can say is that when it comes to sentencing, your co-operation will not go unnoticed. Trust me, Mr McPherson, you've done the right thing.'

Uncertain if her feeling towards McPherson was sympathy for an inept pugilist desperately trying to eke out a living, or pity for a grown man clearly struggling with issues of self-confidence, West, yearning for a large, stiff drink, leaned across the desk and fixed him with a compassionate gaze.

'Alright, Craig,' she said. 'Final question. Why? Why is your mate Nevin framing you for the murder of Nancy Wilson?'

'I've no idea,' said McPherson with a limp shrug of the shoulders. 'I've not done anything to offend him, at least not that I'm aware of.'

'Well, what's the one thing that the three of you have in common? You, Miss Wilson, and Nevin?'

McPherson pondered before answering.

'No, sorry,' he said. 'Is it that she was a boxer as well?'

West, trying her best not to laugh, closed he eyes and smiled.

'Come on,' she said, shaking her head, 'you can do better than that. What on earth have we just been talking about?'

'The money?'

'Good grief!' said Munro. 'I know you took a hammering in the ring, laddie, but it didnae turn you in to a simpleton! Of course it's the blasted money! The question is, how did Nevin know about it?'

McPherson, looking as confused as a chameleon in a bowlful of Skittles, squinted at Munro and frowned as if plagued by a troublesome bout of constipation.

'I told him!' he said. 'That's it! I must have told him.'

'Just like that?'

'No, no,' said McPherson. 'I'm not stupid! I mean, it's not the kind of thing you just drop into a conversation now, is it? No, I must have had a few bevvies, that's for sure.'

'So you were blootered when you blabbed about the money?'

'Aye. Let me think, where were we now? I know, The Bruce Hotel, Newton Stewart. There was the three of us. I remember because when they left I got a wee bit lairy and the landlord called the police. Fair play, I was out of order.'

'Hold on,' said West. 'Three of you? Who else was there?'

'One of Nevin's pals.'

'Did you know him?'

'No,' said McPherson, 'I'd never seen him before and I hope I never do again.'

'Why's that?'

'Because I can't stand freeloaders. He didn't buy a drink all night, not once. He had a habit of disappearing to the gents or taking a phone call whenever it was his round.'

'Do you remember his name?' said West.

'Iain, I think.'

'And what was he doing there?'

'They'd been to watch the football,' said McPherson, 'Annan Athletic, that's their team. They were playing Stranraer.'

'Okay, let's get back to Nevin,' said West. 'What did you tell him? Can you remember what you told Nevin about the money?'

'Aye, I can,' said McPherson. 'He was in dour mood, see, because he never got to see his wean, that's because his ex wouldn't allow it, and he reckoned it was down to the fact that he was permanently skint. I think he was a wee bit jealous too because I had a few quid in my pocket.

Anyway, I told him to relax. I said I knew where I could get my hands on a hundred grand.'

'You must have made his night.'

'Right enough, after that it was like cash for questions. He went on and on, so I thought: what the hell, why not? I told him where it was and I said if he was up for giving me a hand retrieving it then I'd cut him in, but only on condition that we do it properly.'

'Properly?'

'Aye. Leave no trail.'

'So he knew about the safe?'

'He did,' said McPherson, 'but I didn't tell him where it was. I said we can pinch the cash but we open the safe, take it, and lock it up again. All we had to do first was find the code.'

'And had you any idea where Miss Wilson had hidden this code?'

'No. I just assumed it was in that envelope Galbraith gave me to give to her.'

'But Nevin couldnae wait, could he?' said Munro. 'He got impatient and went looking for the code himself, and when Miss Wilson refused to tell him where it was, he lost his rag and pummelled her to death.'

'Which is why,' said West, 'he went round to her gaff afterwards and ripped the place apart looking for it.'

McPherson, amused that he could be party to such a scenario, leaned back in his seat and, much to West's disgust, ran his fingers through his lanky red hair.

'It's unbelievable really,' he said, 'I mean, I always thought he was a half decent fella, a good pal.'

'Well, you obviously don't know him as well as you think,' said West. 'Because if you did, you'd know he had a history of violence, especially against women.'

'Oh well, that would explain his aggression in the ring then. So, what happens now? Am I still going to court?'

'You certainly are,' said Munro, 'but not here. You'll be going to Dumfries. We'll get you sorted soon enough.'

* * *

Bemused that she'd somehow been responsible for nailing a gentleman by the name of Craig McPherson for a crime she knew nothing about, West, feeling as ragged as a road sweeper after a Hogmanay Hootenanny, shuffled slowly up the stairs and stopped outside the office.

'You're looking tired,' said Munro. 'You need a wee sit-down.'

'I should be saying that to you.'

'Och, there's nothing wrong with me, lassie, I'm indefatigable. Aye, that's the word, indefatigable.'

'Of course you are,' said West. 'I don't suppose you're hungry too?'

'It might be lunchtime but I cannae partake, not just yet. I must telephone DCI Clark in Dumfries and give him the good news.'

'It's alright for you, you've got a right result. I still need to collar mine.'

'And you will, Charlie. You will.'

'So, what happens now?'

'Well, I'm not sure about you,' said Munro, 'but I need to get myself a copy of that tape and as for tonight, I shall be pouring myself a large Balvenie. A very special, twenty-one-year-old, port-finished, Balvenie.'

Chapter 14

Senses heightened by the tantalising aroma of southern fried chicken, crispy French fries, and freshly brewed coffee, West, feeling as hollow as a kettle drum, scoured the office until her eyes came to rest on Dougal's desk.

'Oh, you diamond!' she said. 'Did you get some for me?'

'Sorry, miss, I thought you'd be ages yet.'

'Just my luck, all these interviews have given me a raging appetite; honestly, suddenly it's like working in a bleeding recruitment agency.'

'Will a brew and a biscuit do you?'

'It's going to have to. Have you heard from Duncan yet?'

'Aye, you've just missed him,' said Dougal. 'He's on his way back but he's stopping for a bite to eat first.'

'Why is everybody eating except me?'

'It happens to the best of us, miss. Are you sure about that biscuit? I could nip out and get you something.'

'No, it's alright,' said West, 'I haven't got time but thanks anyway. Did you get hold of Nevin?'

'Aye, he's in the custody suite.'

'Good. Then I should get going. I've got a feeling this isn't going to be as straightforward as it seems.'

'Well, if you need some ammo,' said Dougal, 'your star pupil's got a barrel load of bullets for you.'

'Star pupil?'

'Duncan!'

'No need to be facetious,' said West. 'He's just finding his feet. At last. So, what's he got?'

'Jake Nevin, miss, he used to be Lea's…'

'You mean McPherson.'

'Aye okay then – McPherson. Jake Nevin used to be McPherson's sparring partner at the boxing club.'

'Thank you God!'

'And according to the owner,' said Dougal, 'the pair of them were great pals. Nevin even gave him a lift to and from the gym twice a week on the back of the bike.'

'Bingo! So that explains the red hair in the crash helmet.'

'Aye, it does indeed.'

'Which means all we have to do now is find something that actually places Nevin inside the leisure centre at the time of Wilson's attack.'

'Oh, that's not going to be easy,' said Dougal. 'I mean, the fella on the CCTV looks like Nevin, I'll give you that, but I can't get a decent enough image of his face to identify him as such and besides, even if I could, it wouldn't actually prove that he did it.'

'Maybe not,' said West, 'but we'll find something, don't you worry. Even if I have to get down on my hands and knees and comb that leisure centre myself, we'll find something. Now, not that I want to tempt fate or anything like that, but we need to celebrate, for Jimbo's sake if nothing else.'

'That's a grand idea,' said Dougal, 'let's face it, for someone who's meant to be retired he's not gone off the boil, has he? Have you anything in mind?'

'I certainly have. Do me a favour and Google "Balvenie" for me, would you? I want a twenty-one-year-old with a port finish.'

'Right you are. And is there a reason why you're after that particular one?'

'Yup. Jimbo's got a bottle at home and I don't want him sloping off to Carsethorn to drink it on his lonesome. We can all have a few drams here, the four of us, then he can kip at mine.'

'Nice one,' said Dougal. 'Thanks very much.'

'So would you mind popping out and getting a bottle?'

'No bother, but I'll be needing some cash or your credit card.'

'What? For a bottle of whisky?'

'It's not just any whisky,' said Dougal, 'it's one hundred and thirty-five pound's worth of whisky.'

'Holy flipping… sod that! Get a twelve-year-old, he won't know the difference.'

* * *

With the poise of a couch potato who'd had his television set stolen from under his very eyes, Nevin, on the verge of falling asleep, sat with his arms folded and his legs outstretched as West, looking as haggard as a pit pony, pulled up a chair.

Taking a moment to gather her thoughts, she leaned back, pushed both hands against the desk, and fixed Nevin with a vacuous stare.

'I'd barely got through the door,' he said, rubbing his eyes, 'then you lot come and drag me back again. What's going on?'

'There's been a development,' said West, her finger hovering above the voice recorder. 'Still, at least you've had time to shower and grab a change of clothes.'

'Aye, and that's about all I had time for.'

'For the benefit of the tape the time is 3:25 pm. I am Detective Inspector West and also present is Mr John Nevin. You like to keep in shape, don't you John?'

'I prefer Jake.'

'We'll stick to your real name if you don't mind. So, let's start again. You like to work out, don't you? You know, pop down the gym, pump some iron, is that right?'

'No,' said Nevin. 'It's not. I don't need a gym to stay in shape, my work keeps me fit.'

'Does it, really? I never knew you could burn calories just by riding around on a lawnmower.'

'There's more to it than that. There's a lot of graft involved: hedge trimming, tree clearance, shifting stuff. Why the sudden interest?'

'Oh, just curious,' said West. 'I was talking to a mate of mine and he told me that apart from swimming, one of the best ways to keep fit and watch your weight was boxing.'

'Is that so?'

'Yup. Apparently, it's got everything; there's the physical exertion, the various breathing exercises, it's cardiovascular and it sharpens your reflexes too.'

'Sounds magic,' said Nevin. 'Maybe you should give it a go.'

'Yeah, maybe I will. I don't suppose you know of any decent boxing clubs, do you?'

'No. Not me.'

'Really? You do surprise me.'

'How so?'

'Well, for a start,' said West, 'you used to be a regular at The Doonhamers, didn't you?'

Flinching at the sound of the name, Nevin uncrossed his legs and sat up straight.

'That was a long time ago,' he said.

'I know the years have a habit of flying by,' said West, 'but it wasn't that long ago really, was it? Five years perhaps? Six maybe?'

Nevin placed a hand on his chin and regarded West like a chess player contemplating his next move.

'Okay,' he said. 'So I used to box. It's not a crime, is it?'

'No, of course not!' said West. 'I'm just trying to get a handle on it, that's all. I mean, it must be quite an atmosphere with all that testosterone floating about. I imagine there's a great sense of camaraderie, probably a great social life too.'

'Boxing,' said Nevin, narrowing his eyes, 'is all about one on one. Winners and losers. Love and hate. There is no social life, that's why I liked it.'

'Nah. I don't believe you,' said West. 'I don't think you're as much of a loner as you like to make out, I mean, I've heard you used to go to the club with a mate of yours. You even gave him a lift there and back on the back of your bike. Surely you'd have had a few beers after you'd knocked seven bells out of each other?'

'I have no idea who you're talking about,' said Nevin. 'I told you, I've not been for years.'

'Then allow me to refresh your memory because it's Craig we're talking about. Craig McPherson.'

'Christ, Craig McPherson?'

'Yeah. Do you still keep in touch?'

'No. I've not seen him since I quit the gym.'

'So you've no idea what he's been up to?'

'None.'

'And you've no idea where he lives?'

'No.'

'Then you're obviously not aware that he's been living under an assumed name?'

'I'm not with you,' said Nevin. 'What do you mean *an assumed name*?'

'I mean,' said West impatiently, 'that ever since he left Palnackie, he's been living as Rupert Lea.'

'Good for him, but like I say, I've not seen him.'

West took a deep breath, tousled her hair, and sighed.

'Funny that,' she said with a bemused smile, 'because he says otherwise. In fact, he told us that he's only just bought a motorcycle off you.'

'If you say so.'

'Oh it's not just me saying so. And it's not just McPherson, or should I say Lea. It's the DVLA too. They've got the log book and it's got your name and your address on it. And guess what? They're changing it to his.'

'Well, whatever he's calling himself,' said Nevin. 'It makes no difference to me.'

West hauled herself to her feet, pushed the chair to one side, and leaned against the wall with her hands in her pockets.

'I'm tired,' she said, staring at the floor. 'I'm tired of going around in circles, I'm tired of being nice, and I'm tired of dealing with arseholes who think they're smart, so how about I just charge you now and get it over with? That way I can hold you a bit longer, it might give you time to come your senses.'

Nevin scowled at West and raised a hand.

'Now hold on,' he said, 'let's not be hasty! Look, I've not been entirely straight with you, okay? The truth is we did keep in touch and aye, I sold him a bike, but I still don't see why it's such a big deal.'

'I'll tell you why, shall I?' said West. 'Because as far as deals go, this one really is pretty big. You see, we've got someone who looks like you, and your motorbike, outside the leisure centre the day Miss Wilson was murdered…'

'I told you, I'm not one for getting up early…'

'…and that was before you sold the bike to McPherson.'

'…and if I was there, then I was probably collecting my wages.'

West glanced at Nevin and smiled.

'Let's use that as euphemism, shall we?' she said. 'It sounds a lot nicer than "murder". So, after you'd *collected your wages*, I think you rode the bike round to McPherson's gaff and dumped it in his garden.'

'Aye, of course I did,' said Nevin sarcastically. 'And I stopped to fill it up with petrol on the way.'

'Then I think you went inside and dropped off a few odds and sods – spanners, waterproofs, gloves, helmet, that sort of thing.'

'You're absolutely right, I can't deny it! And I had a huge bag on my back to get it all there.'

'That's what I thought!' said West. 'Like a rucksack! One of those big rucksacks with loads of compartments and straps and little pockets on the side, you know the kind, just big enough to hold a camera.'

Nevin paused, glanced furtively around the room, then grinned as if he'd just remembered the answer to a particularly fiendish question in a pub quiz.

'A camera!' he said. 'Because I wanted a wee selfie with the bike before I left it?'

'Nah, you're not that sentimental,' said West. 'You couldn't give a stuff about the bike, but you took the camera so you could transfer all those lovely photos of Nancy Wilson onto McPherson's computer.'

'Did I not steal all his passwords as well?'

'I give up,' said West. 'Like I said, I'm tired and we've got your fingerprints all over the camera.'

'Well, you would have, wouldn't you?' said Nevin, smiling smugly, 'but it doesn't prove a thing. I found the camera in his room so I thought I'd have a wee nosey, you know, see what he'd been taking photos of.'

'Is that so?'

'Aye. It is. Right, now we've cleared that up, it's time I was leaving, you've taken up too much of my time already.'

'Stay where you are,' said West. 'You're not going anywhere.'

'Oh aye? How so?'

'Because at the risk of repeating myself, I'm charging you. Again.'

'You have got to be joking! What is it this time?'

'Same as before,' said West. 'Don't worry, we've kept your cell nice and warm for you. Now, you sit tight and someone will show you to your room.'

Chapter 15

Unlike the glowing, whisky-flushed cheeks of a mawkish mourner at an open-topped wake, Duncan, looking as pale as a pint of rum eggnog, owed his pallid complexion to an unprecedented lack of sleep, whilst Dougal, who worked by moonlight, blamed his own ghostly pallor on a vitamin D deficiency and hypersensitivity to sunlight.

Deeming them both as dour as a pair of inebriates at a Temperance Society meeting, Munro, bemoaning their lack of stamina, smiled benignly and placed a packet of chocolate fingers between them.

'Sugar,' he said. 'It'll do you good.'

'Thanks very much,' said Dougal. 'Have you not got some evidence to go with that?'

'By jiminy, you're like a couple of Colleens complaining about your stilettos! If you'd had yourself some porridge for breakfast, you'd not be flagging now!'

'The only flag I'm waving, chief, is a white one,' said Duncan. 'I'm pure shattered.'

'And I'd rather be booking my season ticket for the fishing at Kilbirnie Loch,' said Dougal. 'I'm in need of a break myself.'

Munro took a seat, helped himself to a biscuit, and snapped it in half.

'Have you ever thought of entering one of those quiz shows on the television?' he said. 'You know, like that "Millionaire" for example?'

'No,' said Dougal. 'I have not.'

'Good. Because you'd fail. Okay, the clock's ticking, let's start afresh. What's the problem?'

'Oh chief, you know what the problem is,' said Duncan. 'We've nothing concrete on that Nevin fella.'

'Aye, but it's not that that's bothering me,' said Dougal. 'It's the fact that any second now West is going to come through that door and tell us to take ourselves off to the leisure centre on another pointless treasure hunt. She'll have us crawling about that ceiling like a couple of rats scavenging for titbits.'

'And is that a problem?' said Munro. 'Because from where I'm sitting, I'd say that's exactly what you're paid to do.'

'Aye, maybe so,' said Duncan, 'but not after a shift like this; it's bordering on slave labour.'

Munro, tickled by the irreverent jibe, allowed himself a wry smile and sipped his tea.

'Far be it for me to interfere in your investigation,' he said, 'but would you care to know what a retired old fool like myself thinks of your dilemma?'

'I'm all ears,' said Duncan. 'Fire away.'

'Okay. If you're sitting comfortably, then I'll begin. Correct me if I'm wrong, but did you not say that Nevin, if indeed he is the perpetrator, disabled the CCTV in the evening? After all the other staff had left?'

'It would appear so, aye.'

'And the motorbike you've a fixation with, when did that appear?'

'First thing in the morning,' said Dougal. 'About fifteen minutes before the cleaners arrived to open up shop.'

'So the assumption is that Nevin arrived early, gained access to the building courtesy of the cleaners and was there all day, hiding out until he had a chance to be alone with Miss Wilson?'

'Aye, that's pretty much it,' said Dougal. 'It's the only explanation.'

'Is it?' said Munro as he drained his mug. 'Is it indeed?'

Likening the brace of battle-weary detectives to a couple of short-sighted lumberjacks in a forest full of Scots pine, Munro walked to the back of the room and, addressing the window rather than his audience, cynically shook his head and smiled.

'Can you not see it?' he said. 'By jiminy, it's as plain as the nose on your face!'

'If you're about to crack this, chief,' said Duncan with a yawn, 'then don't hold back. Let's have it with both barrels.'

'Why?' said Munro. 'Why would Nevin turn up first thing in the morning and lie low the entire day before attacking Miss Wilson? Why did he not show up five minutes before they closed?'

'Well,' said Dougal, 'because other folk would've seen him arrive. There would have been witnesses. They might have asked themselves the question: what's he doing here at this time of day?'

'Close,' said Munro, 'but no cigar. You see, laddie, this Nevin fellow isnae stupid. He's gone out of his way to frame McPherson for the murder and he's thought it through.'

'How so?'

'Good grief, do I have to spell it out? See here, he's of a similar height and build to McPherson, okay? That was the crucial element in his plan if he was to succeed in getting the likes of you to chase your own tails.'

'Go on.'

'So he turns up on a motorcycle he's already sold to McPherson knowing that the DVLA would verify the sale, and he makes sure that his face is hidden from view when he enters the building, but here's the thing – he's a legitimate employee of the leisure centre, is he not?'

'Aye,' said Duncan. 'He is.'

'Then why the blazes would he have to hide? No, no,' said Munro, 'I'll tell you what he did. He entered the building, changed out of his motorcycle gear and wandered about the place doing whatever it is he does in full view of everyone and nobody batted an eyelid.'

'Makes perfect sense to me, chief, but I'll tell you this for nothing, Westy's not going like it, she's not going to like it at all.'

'There's only two things I don't like,' said West as she plodded through the door. 'Broccoli and bananas, and as this isn't "Gardeners Question Time" you must be talking about something else, so come on, let's have it.'

'After you, chief,' said Duncan with a sardonic smile. 'I've got my career to think of.'

* * *

Listening to Munro's interpretation of events like a disheartened teenager on the cusp of learning that her trip to Disneyland had been cancelled, West, in an unexpected show of positivity, conceded that contrary to her own beliefs, he was probably right.

'Well, it's certainly feasible, Jimbo,' she said, 'there's no doubt about it but even if he was a regular at the centre, then unless he had good reason to be there, I still say he'd have raised a few eyebrows. And I still think he might have been better off tucking himself away until he was ready to pounce.'

'Well, that's your call, Charlie,' said Munro, 'and you must do what you think is right. So tell me, what are you going to do?'

'Please don't suggest anything involving stepladders,' said Dougal. 'I'm not good with heights.'

'Numpty,' said Duncan, struggling to keep his eyes open, 'that's not necessary now. All we have to do is take ourselves off to the centre and question everyone who was working that day and if they saw Nevin wandering about the place then we simply ask them what he was doing.'

'There you go,' said West, 'simple when you know how! Right, so who's going…'

'Sorry, miss,' said Duncan as he raised a hand, 'but it's too late for that. There's a lot of part-timers down there and they'll be done for the day now.'

'You're as slippery as an eel, you know that? But you're right, so we'll concentrate on something else instead. We'll concentrate on finding that vital bit of something which will nail Nevin to the cross.'

'And have you any idea what this vital bit of something looks like?' said Dougal.

'Buggered if I know,' said West. 'I need to sleep on it, or better still, drink on it. Dougal's got a treat in store so we can all toast Jimbo's success.'

'Aye, nice one,' said Duncan. 'I've got to hand it to you, chief, you did well to collar that McPherson fella, and Galbraith too.'

'Credit where it's due,' said Munro, 'it wasnae all down to me, I did have some help.'

'So,' said West, 'who's for a dram?'

'Oh not for me,' said Dougal, 'I'll take a juice, me and alcohol don't get along.'

'And I've a drive ahead of me,' said Duncan. 'Destination duvet.'

'Oh well,' said West, 'looks like it's just you and me then, Jimbo. We'll have a snifter then you can crash at mine.'

'Put the cap back on, Charlie, you're driving too.'

'Me?'

'Aye, I'm convalescing, remember.'

* * *

147

Under the tutelage of his late wife, Munro had soon discovered the benefits of employing a "clean as you go" technique when toiling in the kitchen or for that matter when executing any task which involved a degree of detritus, whilst West, without the guidance of a spouse, partner, or parent, deployed the much simpler but ultimately more arduous method of utilising every available piece of crockery in the house until forced to face a mountain of grime-coated utensils armed with a bottle of detergent and a despondent sigh.

Dumping the carrier bags on the dining table, she tossed her coat to the floor, grabbed two tumblers from the drainer and uncorked the Balvenie as a weary Munro, in dire need of a seat and some sustenance, glanced towards the kitchen and gawped at the array of pots and pans wallowing in the sink, the crusty plates piled high on the counter, the charred griddle pan sitting on the hob, and the oven trays coated in a fine layer of oil.

'Jumping Jehoshaphat!' he said. 'If you were a restaurant you'd be closed down!'

'You what?'

'I'll be needing a chisel to scrape the muck off these plates.'

'It's not my fault,' said West, 'I've been busy. Besides, when I studied Home Economics at school, we concentrated on the cooking aspect, not how to deal with the aftermath of a culinary disaster.'

'If you were a dictionary definition, Charlie,' said Munro as he rolled up his sleeves, 'you'd be the antonym of *domestic goddess*.'

'Thanks very much.'

'No wonder you were so keen to get a takeaway.'

'Alright, stop having a go!' said West. 'I'll do it now. You sit down and have yourself a relaxing aspirin.'

'Well, if you insist,' said Munro as he sipped his whisky, 'I'll not argue. By the way, I forgot to ask, how was Nevin when you booked him this afternoon?'

'Still as stubborn as ever,' said West. 'He's not budging. Any idea how much a dishwasher costs?'

'About eight pounds an hour. Did you mention the money? The fact that McPherson told us all about it?'

'No. I thought I'd keep that one up my sleeve and play it as my trump card. I meant to buy.'

'I've no idea,' said Munro, 'but I'd wager it's substantially more than a bottle of Fairy Liquid.'

West flicked on the oven, returned a gleaming griddle pan to the hob and pulled two ten-ounce sirloins from a carrier bag.

'My turn,' she said. 'You've still got some explaining to do.'

'How so?'

'Don't play the innocent with me, Jimbo; for hijacking one of my team to aid your own private investigation.'

'Och, that!' said Munro. 'It was nothing, Charlie. No, I correct myself. It was everything.'

'I'm too tired for riddles, spit it out.'

'I needed a computer to research this Galbraith fellow. You were busy so I telephoned Duncan and he brought me the spare from the office.'

'You mean he drove it down to yours? Christ, no wonder he's knackered.'

'Aye, and he was kind enough to fetch me some groceries along the way and he stopped for the night.'

'He kipped at yours? Why?'

'Well, here's the thing,' said Munro. 'I was that tired, Charlie, I fell asleep, not surprising considering I'd just driven all the way from Kennacraig. Anyway, I awoke at 4 am and he'd done it all for me. I didnae even tell him what I was looking for.'

'Then how did he know?'

'Because he used his brain. He checked my search history on the internet, had a wee peek at my notes, and off he went. I'm telling you Charlie, if it wasnae for

Duncan, Galbraith wouldnae be behind bars and McPherson would still be wandering the streets.'

'You've grown quite fond of him, haven't you?' said West. 'I reckon he reminds you of yourself as a young copper.'

'Perhaps,' said Munro, 'but that's by the by. The bottom line is I can see a spark in him, Charlie, just like I saw a spark in you. All you have to do is fan the flame and watch it grow. Are we not having chips with our supper?'

'They're in the oven. So, what are you saying? About Duncan, I mean.'

'Oh it's not for me to say anything, Charlie. It's your team, not mine.'

'Don't give me that,' said West. 'You know as well I do, they both still think of you as the gaffer.'

'You underestimate yourself, lassie. I'm simply saying you should give the lad a chance. Why not put him forward for his exams?'

'And what? End up with two sergeants? Dougal won't be happy.'

'Och, they're like chalk and cheese…'

'Laurel and Hardy more like.'

'…but they work well together. Like a pickled onion and a chunk of cheddar. I think Dougal will enjoy sharing the responsibility.'

'Yeah, okay,' said West. 'I'll think about it. Wine?'

'Aye of course, but I'll have a clean glass, please.'

* * *

Reminded of a wildlife documentary featuring a pride of lions on the Serengeti devouring an unlucky wildebeest, West, refraining from commenting on table manners, watched as Munro ripped into his steak as though it were his last meal on earth.

'Are you sure you should be eating that?' she said.

'Why not?'

'Nothing. Just all that cholesterol, that's all.'

'Are you a doctor now?'

'No.'

'I thought not,' said Munro with a wink, 'because if you were, you'd know that the cholesterol in this steak was superbly balanced by copious amounts of iron and the vitamins B6 and B12...'

'That's me told then.'

'...not to mention the magnesium, which is essential in regulating blood pressure. So, lecture over, what's next with Nevin?'

'Apart from the obvious?' said West. 'Dunno. If nothing turns up, I might have to wing it on the evidence we've got and see what the fiscal says.'

'It might work,' said Munro, 'but what you have is largely circumstantial and you'd be running the risk of seeing him walk away scot-free if she doesnae think the case has legs.'

'I know, I know. Which is why first thing tomorrow we're going to check in with Dougal, then head off up to the leisure centre.'

'We?'

'Yup. I want you to cast your eye over the murder scene, retrace his steps, that kind of thing. You never know, you might spot something we've missed.'

'Aye, okay then,' said Munro, 'but I'm telling you now, Charlie, I'm not crawling around a ceiling, do I make myself clear?'

Chapter 16

Since the demise of his first ever long term relationship – a two-week dalliance with a mousey but insatiable law student with a minimalist wardrobe and a fondness for Smirnoff Ice – Dougal, who preferred the unconditional love of a brown trout and the solitude of a deserted riverbank, had gladly returned to the life of a singleton, free from the woes of worrying over what to say, what to wear, and what to drink.

Comforted by the familiarity of his computer, he sat scrutinising the photographs of McPherson's XT500 on one screen whilst procuring a season's fishing at Kilbirnie Loch on the other when West, looking as bright as a button in her black jeans and crisp, white T-shirt, breezed through the door and plonked one tea, two cappuccinos, and three bacon baps on the desk.

'You're early, miss,' he said. 'Is the boss not with you?'

'I certainly am,' said Munro, trailing in her wake, 'but not for long. We're away to the leisure centre just as soon as I've had a word with your superior about installing a chair lift.'

'What are you up to?' said West. 'Anything interesting?'

'Aye, maybe. I've been looking over the photos the SOCOs sent of McPherson's bike…'

'The bike? I thought you were done with all that. The scratches and stuff?'

'So did I,' said Dougal, 'but I see now that the steering lock's broken and the ignition wires are hanging loose.'

'And what does that mean exactly?'

'It means it can be started without a key. Just jump on the kick start and give it some welly.'

'So you think Nevin might have nicked it before selling it on?'

'Not according to the DVLA,' said Dougal. 'Nevin was the legal owner right enough. The only thing I can think of is that he lost the keys so he disabled the ignition.'

'Isn't that a bit risky?' said West. 'Wouldn't that make it easy to pinch?'

'I doubt anyone would be interested. It's twenty-three years old.'

'Don't make them like they used to, eh?'

'Oh and by the way, McLeod's on his way over.'

'Andy? He's coming all the way from Glasgow?'

'No,' said Dougal, 'he's been doing a post-mortem over at University Hospital Crosshouse. He'll not be long.'

'Well, what does he want here?'

'You, I imagine.'

'Steady.'

'Anything else?'

'Aye there is,' said Dougal. 'You'll like this, boss, I finally got my hands on Wilson's CV. The manageress at the centre sent it over.'

'Is it not a bit late for that, laddie?'

'Maybe, but at least it does provide us with a back-story.'

'Aye, quite right,' said Munro, 'indeed it does. Apologies for being so hasty.'

'Not necessary. Will I fill you in?'

'Yeah, go on,' said West. 'Let's see what the poor girl's been up to.'

'Okay, according to this, she's been single since forever, enjoys outdoor pursuits and organic food, and she also supports the WWF.'

'She's into wrestling?'

Dougal glanced at Munro and rolled his eyes.

'The World Wide Fund for Nature, miss.'

'Of course it is,' said West. 'Silly me. Carry on.'

'Before taking up the post in Auchinleck, she was a swimming instructor in Maybole and before that at the Annan Academy. Education wise, she attended Dumfries and Galloway college where she gained an HNC and then an HND in "Coaching and Developing Sport", but this is where it gets interesting.'

'About time,' said West, tossing him a sandwich. 'Here, dive in before it goes cold.'

'Did you get one for me?'

West turned to face the grinning, willowy figure hovering in the doorway and smiled.

'Sorry,' she said as McLeod pulled up a chair. 'If I'd known you were coming… I could make you a brew if you like?'

'Thanks,' said McLeod, 'very much appreciated. 'And how are you, James? I hear you went under the knife recently?'

'I did indeed,' said Munro. 'Nothing serious, the pump was suffering from a wee bit of wear and tear, that's all. They gave it a clean-up and changed a couple of parts so it's fine now.'

'Well, just remember, you might be firing on all cylinders now but you still need to take it easy. Not too much exercise, and are you watching your diet?'

'You know me,' said Munro as he slipped a napkin over his toastie, 'never one to ignore the advice of doctors.'

'I'm glad to hear it. So you're cutting back on the red meat and getting plenty of fresh vegetables?'

'Aye of course! Green beans, you cannae beat them.'

West, smirking as Munro squirmed in his chair, handed McLeod a mug of tea.

'Here you go,' she said. 'Now, I don't want to sound rude but we're a bit pushed for time this morning so if you've come to give us an update on the beard it's going to have to wait, okay?'

'Charming as ever,' said McLeod. 'Actually, I was wondering where you were with the Wilson case.'

'Nearly there, why?'

'Because that's what I've come about.'

Seizing what might be his only opportunity, Munro slipped the bacon roll into his pocket and answered the call of his phone.

'I have to take this,' he said as he made for the door, 'it's DCI Clark, you carry on without me.'

* * *

As one of the enviable few who could force an all-you-can-eat buffet into administration in a single sitting, West, in an uncharacteristic display of magnanimity, split her toastie in two and handed half to McLeod as Duncan, looking none the worse for wear, ambled through the door.

'Aye, aye,' he said, 'all present and correct, I see. Mr McLeod, you okay pal?'

'Very well, thanks. And yourself?'

'Aye, not bad. A good night's sleep makes all the difference.'

'Have you been burning the candle?' said McLeod. 'Or has Charlie been overworking you again?'

'No, no. I've been overworking myself. Stretching the old brain cells a bit too far. So, what's the story?'

'Andy's come to fill us in on the Wilson case,' said West. 'At least I think he has.'

'Well, don't let me stop you,' said Duncan. 'I'm going to stick the kettle on.'

McLeod took a folded sheet of A4 paper from his inside pocket and set it on the table.

'I did email this to you,' he said, 'but you've obviously not got it.'

'What is it?'

'The DNA results from the hair and skin samples I extracted from Wilson's fingernails.'

'That's just what we've been waiting for!' said West elatedly. 'This could be the proof we need to put Nevin away once and for all! What? Why the face?'

'What face?' said McLeod.

'Your face. You look, I don't know, puzzled.'

'Do I? No reason.'

'I'm beginning to get a bad feeling about this,' said West. 'Just to be clear, the samples you sent for analysis, if they did throw up a match, then it would definitely be the perpetrator, right? I mean, there's no other way that stuff could have got there?'

'None,' said McLeod. 'The fragments were too deeply embedded. What's more the skin still had a moisture content which, in terms of a time-frame, would match the time of the attack. Oh, and I also found a tiny sample of blood.'

'So she definitely put up a fight?'

'Absolutely,' said McLeod, 'and a good one too. In fact there's every chance her assailant still has scratch marks on the top of his head.'

'Right then,' said West, 'down to business. The reason you're here, obviously, is because you have got a match.'

'Correct.'

West stared at McLeod and took a deep breath.

'Okay,' she said, 'in that case, the name we're looking for – the name we need – is John Nevin.'

McLeod unfolded the sheet of paper, glanced furtively at Dougal, then at Duncan, and pursed his lips.

'Sorry,' he said, shaking his head. 'It's not Nevin.'

West, her face a picture of disappointment and fear, froze for a moment and contemplated her prospects as a check-out girl, before exploding like a firecracker, sending Dougal diving for cover.

'For crying out loud!' she said as she thumped the desk. 'What do you mean, it's not Nevin?'

'Exactly that, Charlie. It's no-one called Nevin.'

'Okay, okay. If it's not him then it has to be a geezer called McPherson. Craig McPherson.'

'No.'

West glared at McLeod, held his gaze, then cracked a maniacal grin and cocked her head.

'I've got it,' she said calmly. 'It's a simple mix-up, right? McPherson's been living under an assumed name and that's the one you've got. It's Rupert Lea.'

'Three strikes,' said McLeod. 'Sorry.'

West leapt from her seat, slammed the chair under the desk and stormed across the room sending a wastepaper basket to the wall courtesy of a well-aimed kick from her reinforced boot.

'Well, who in God's name is it?' she said, yelling as she raised her arms. 'Who?'

McLeod, impressed by the fiery yet hitherto unseen side to her personality, sat back and smiled.

'If it helps,' he said softly, 'it's a fella by the name of Iain Fraser.'

'Who? I've never heard of him! Who the hell is Iain Fraser? And why is he on the DB?'

'Sorry, Charlie. I'm afraid I can't help you there.'

'I can,' said Dougal as his fingers flew across the keyboard. 'Fraser you say? If he's on the database then he's got form. Here we go. Iain Fraser. He lives in Cargenbridge, just outside Dumfries. He was done for assaulting a police officer and he got three months.'

'And why the bleeding hell did he punch a copper?'

'Celtic – Rangers match. Say no more.'

'Get him picked up! Now!'

* * *

Dusting crumbs from his chest, Munro, perturbed by the racket emanating from the office, eased open the door and scowled at West.

'I could hear just the one voice along the corridor,' he said. 'And that was yours, Charlie. What on earth is going on?'

'We know who killed Nancy Wilson!'

'Aye, we do indeed.'

'And now we have the evidence to prove it.'

'Excellent. That means we'll not be troubling ourselves with a trip to the leisure centre then.'

'There's just one problem.'

'Life wouldnae be the same without one. What is it?'

'It's not who we think it is. It's not Nevin.'

'Dear, dear. That is a shame,' said Munro. 'And judging by the looks on your faces, I'm guessing the perpetrator doesnae have red hair either?'

'No! He bleeding well does not!'

'So, it's not McPherson.'

'No!' said West. 'It's some bloke called Iain Fraser! I've never heard of Iain Fraser! Where the hell did he come from?'

Munro crossed his arms, stared pensively at the ceiling, and rubbed his chin.

'Fraser,' he said, almost whispering. 'Now, where have I heard that name before?'

'Oh here we go!' said West. 'The sage of Caledonia's about to explain everything!'

'Do you know what they say about sarcasm being the lowest form of wit, Charlie?'

'What about it?'

'I disagree entirely. I think it's the funniest if not the cleverest form of humour there is. Iain Fraser. He's the fellow who found Flora MacDonald halfway up the chimney.'

'Are you serious?' said West. 'I mean, are you absolutely sure?'

'One hundred percent, lassie. He's the fellow who's been tasked with renovating her cottage, that's why the name's so familiar.'

With the atmosphere as still as a Remembrance Day service at Saint Margaret's Cathedral, Duncan, completely unfazed by the turn of events, swung his feet onto the desk and broke the silence with a satisfying slurp of his tea.

'So, if it was this Fraser fella chasing the money,' he said, 'then it stands to reason the only way he could've known about it was either through Galbraith or…'

'God, I've been so stupid!' said West. 'Jimbo! McPherson said there were three of them in the pub, remember? He said Nevin's mate was called Iain!'

'Aye, indeed he did,' said Munro, 'so you need to ask him if he cannae remember the fellow's surname or at the very least give you a description. In fact, if you've a wee photo of this Fraser chap, that may be all you need to jog his memory. Either way, if I were you, I'd take myself off to Dumfries as soon as possible.'

'Roger that,' said Duncan. 'I fancy a wee blast down the motorway.'

'Give me a minute,' said Dougal, 'and I'll print you off a photo.'

'I'm going to have a quick word with Nevin about his relationship with Fraser,' said West. 'It seems to me the two of them were in this together.'

'And I'll take that as my cue to leave,' said McLeod. 'Best of luck, Charlie.'

'Yeah, thanks Andy. I'll give you a buzz once this is all done and dusted. Dougal, get yourself down to incoming please, and take Fraser to the interview room as soon as he arrives. Jimbo, you meet me there, I need someone to scare the pants off him.'

Chapter 17

'For the benefit of the tape, I'm DI West, also present is DS McCrae and James Munro. Would you state your name, please?'

'Iain Fraser.'

'Do you understand why you're here, Mr Fraser?'

Fraser reached into his pocket, pulled out a pouch of tobacco and, hands trembling, rolled a cigarette.

'I do. Aye.'

'And have you got a lawyer or would you like us to appoint a duty solicitor for you?'

'No, you're alright.'

'Good,' said West. 'Then we'll continue. Now, unlike anything you might have seen on the TV, I'm not going to run around in circles trying to trip you up or shout at you until your ears bleed. The bottom line is we have irrefutable evidence that you were responsible for the death of Miss Nancy Wilson, so is there anything you'd like to say?'

Fraser glanced at Munro and raised his eyebrows.

'The wife will be livid,' he said. 'She doesn't know I'm here yet.'

Returning Fraser's expression with the subtlest of smiles, Munro, deeming the tactics of the Spanish Inquisition as completely unnecessary, left the desk and walked towards the rear of the room.

'Would you like to call her?' he said, as he came to a halt directly behind him. 'Will she not be worried?'

'Best not. I think I'll wait.'

'As you wish,' said Munro. 'Tell me, Mr Fraser, do you cut your hair yourself? You know, with one of those electric shaver-type things?'

'No. Barber shop. Once a month.'

'Well, I'd sue them if I were you. They've given you a couple of nasty wee nicks atop your head.'

Fraser brushed his hair as if dusting off an imaginary spider.

'Oh that,' he said lamely.

'Aye that,' said Munro. 'You see Mr Fraser, that's the irrefutable evidence we've been talking about. We found your DNA beneath Miss Wilson's fingernails.'

'I see.'

'I see?' said West. 'Is that it? No protest? No "you've got the wrong man?" No "I'm innocent?"'

'What's the point?'

'So you admit it?'

'Aye,' said Fraser hanging his head. 'In my defence though…'

'You have no defence, not now.'

'…I didn't mean to do it. I thought she could swim.'

'Did you indeed? Well, I've got news for you, she was already dead when she hit the water.'

'What? How so?'

'Because you pummelled her so hard, she suffered a haematoma to the brain.'

'Oh Jesus!' said Fraser, his voice barely a whisper. 'I thought she was… I thought she was still…'

'You should've thought this through, shouldn't you?' said West. 'I mean, I can't see your wife and kids being too enamoured with what you've done, can you?'

'No. They'll not be happy. They'll not be happy at all, but in all fairness, I was doing it for them.'

'Oh please! Don't give me that!'

'No, that came out wrong,' said Fraser, 'but you know what I mean. I did it because we're always struggling.'

'Struggling? Why's that? Have you got a big family?'

'No. Two teenage daughters. That's it.'

'And they're a drain, are they?'

'Same old story,' said Fraser. 'Clothes, phones, pocket money.'

'No different to anyone else, is it?'

'Maybe not, but other folk seem to have the money to pay for it.'

'Does your wife not work?'

'Part-time, but it's not much.'

'I am surprised,' said West. 'From what I hear, you're a talented builder and I thought you lot charged an arm and a leg just for showing up, so is that not enough?'

'Ordinarily, aye,' said Fraser, 'but there's just not the work there used to be.'

'So this seemed like the easy way out?'

'It seemed like one way out. I just thought... I thought if I had some cash then I could treat the wife, take the weans on holiday, they've not even been abroad. Ever.'

'And John Nevin had the answer to all your problems, right? How long have you known him?'

'A few years.'

'And how did you meet?'

'Football.'

'So you're good mates?'

'Not really,' said Fraser. 'More like drinking pals. A couple of pints before the match, and a couple more after.'

'And has Nevin got you involved with anything like this before?'

Fraser looked to the ground, his shoulders heaving as he sighed.

'He's helped me out a few times.'

'How?'

'Just stuff. When I've been strapped for cash and I've needed some new gear.'

'Tools you mean?' said Munro. 'Like a new drill perhaps? Or supplies, like sand and cement?'

'Aye, that kind of thing. They're not cheap when you've not got two pennies to rub together.'

'And did it not cross your mind that the materials he was passing on to you were probably stolen?'

'No questions asked,' said Fraser, 'you know how it works.'

'Aye, I do,' said Munro, 'all too well but this is something altogether different, is it not?'

'He said it would be easy. No hassle, in and out and we'd have a few quid in our pockets.'

'A few quid?' said Munro. 'It's not exactly Brink's-Mat, I'll give you that, but fifty thousand pounds a piece? That's three or four years' salary for some folk.'

'Looks like you've got yourself in a bit of a pickle,' said West, 'but if it makes you feel any better, your mate John Nevin, and his mate Craig McPherson, are both banged up so you may as well give us your side of the story.'

Fraser, who appeared to have aged dramatically in the space of ten minutes, tucked the cigarette behind his ear and rubbed his face with the palms of his hands.

'We'd been to Stranraer,' he said, 'for the football. John had arranged to meet his pal in the pub on the way back. Just a wee bevvy because we were on the bike.'

'And what pal is this?'

'That Craig fella you just mentioned.'

'Go on.'

'John was on a right downer. I thought it was because we'd lost the match but, as soon as he'd got an ale down his neck, he started on about how broke he was and whinging about how he never got to see his kid because his ex wouldn't allow it.'

'So McPherson told him about the money?'

'Not immediately, no,' said Fraser. 'The fella was hammered, I mean, he's like one rung up the ladder from being a jakey. Anyways, eventually he came up with this story about a wee girl who had a hundred thousand quid stashed away in her house. To be honest, I thought he was on a wind-up. I never believed him. I thought he was joking just to shut John up.'

'But he wasn't?'

'I don't know,' said Fraser. 'But John believed him. You should've seen his face light up when he heard the girl's name.'

'And why was that?'

'He couldn't believe his luck. He said he knew her, that they'd been out together a couple of times. He said that this Craig fella was a numpty and that he'd never twig if we took the money for ourselves.'

'Sounds like a nice mate to have,' said West. 'He'd have got on well with Caesar.'

'Who?'

'Never mind. So even though Nevin knew this girl, he wasn't fussed about robbing her? About stealing off his ex-girlfriend?'

'It didn't seem to bother him, no.'

'So you hatched a plan to relieve Miss Wilson of her money?'

'Not me,' said Fraser. 'John. He planned it all. He said she was more likely to tell a stranger where the money was because it would sound odd coming from him. Besides, it was the only way I was going to get a cut.'

'So, what happened?'

'He told me to get myself down to the leisure centre and to wait out of sight until he came to fetch me. That way, I'd know the cameras had been turned off.'

'Go on.'

'He came to the door about nine o'clock and called me over. He gave me a pair of gloves to wear so I wouldn't leave my fingerprints all over the place.'

'And were they motorcycle gloves?' said West. 'Black, leather motorcycle gloves?'

'Aye. They're the ones he uses all the time.'

'So you went inside?'

'Aye. John said I was to wait ten minutes while he softened her up and then I was to head over to the office.'

'And when you got there?'

'They were chatting away like old pals,' said Fraser. 'Having a wee giggle. John had a camera with him and he was taking a few photos.'

Munro leaned back in his seat, folded his arms and fixed Fraser with a steely gaze.

'Did she not get a wee fright?' he said. 'I mean, a total stranger walking into her office after hours, you must have scared her half to death.'

'I did, aye,' said Fraser, 'but John introduced me. He told her he was giving me a lift home on the bike and then she relaxed. She even offered me a drink, a diet Coke.'

'And how long did you stay?' said West. 'I mean before you started laying into her?'

'Not long,' said Fraser. 'John was laying on the charm and I lost my bottle. I got impatient. I just blurted it out. I asked her where the money was and she started to panic.'

'I'm not surprised.'

'The thing is, she thought I was talking about the money from the centre, like a cashbox or something, because she kept saying they didn't keep cash in the building, that all the members had passes. She even offered me her purse and that, I'm ashamed to say, is when I lost my temper. I started throwing things about the place.'

'And your pal Nevin,' said Munro. 'Did he not try to intervene? Did he not try to calm the situation?'

'He did,' said Fraser, 'as best he could. To tell the truth, I think I put the fear of God up him as well. He kept apologising to the girl and trying to push me out the door saying we should leave it.'

'But you couldnae?'

'No.'

'And Nevin?'

'One minute he was there, the next he was gone.'

'So he left you to it?' said West. 'He scarpered and left you alone with Miss Wilson? He left you to carry on beating the living daylights out of her?'

'Aye,' said Fraser. 'God's truth, I don't know why I did it. I don't know what came over me.'

Likening his submissive behaviour to that of a petrified schoolboy worried that his parents might discover he'd been caught red-handed shoplifting half a dozen Mars Bars from the local supermarket, Munro leaned forward and stared inquisitively at Fraser.

'Not that I'm defending your actions,' he said, 'but the human psyche has different ways of reacting to any given situation. Tell me straight, Mr Fraser, apart from one charge of assault, have you ever been accused of acting violently before?'

'No. Never.'

'Are you given to over-reacting in otherwise normal situations, like spilling your tea, perhaps? Or being caught in a traffic jam?'

Fraser chewed his bottom lip as he pondered the question.

'I never used to be,' he said, 'but recently…'

'How recently?'

'The last year or so, I suppose. I've a tendency to fly off the handle for no given reason.'

'And the onset of this behaviour, would this coincide with the onset of your financial woes?'

'Maybe. Aye. Probably.'

'Then I fear your actions might be stress related,' said Munro. 'I think you should have a psychiatric assessment.'

West, befuddled by Munro's new found role as counsel for the defence, cast him a sideways glance and cleared her throat.

'Let's not get side-tracked, eh?' she said. 'So, Mr Fraser, you were throwing a hissy fit in front of Miss Wilson, what happened next?'

'I dragged her from the office to…'

'Hold up! You did what? You dragged her? Forcibly? How?'

'By the collar.'

'And she didn't struggle?'

'Oh she struggled alright,' said Fraser. 'If she could've landed a punch, I swear she could have put me down.'

'And no doubt that riled you even more?'

'I flipped,' said Fraser with a shameful nod. 'I never realised how hard I hit her. Honest, I thought I was giving her a wee tap.'

'Not that it's any consolation,' said West, 'but the gloves wouldn't have helped.'

'How so?'

'Knuckle protectors. Kevlar. You might as well have hit her with a sock full of billiard balls. Right, nearly done Mr Fraser, just one more question for now. When did you see Nevin again?'

'Outside. He was waiting for me outside.'

'And did you tell him what you'd done?'

'I did,' said Fraser. 'He told me to take myself off and keep my head down. He said that he'd sort it and that it would all blow over. That we'd be in the clear.'

'And the gloves?'

'He took them. He said he knew exactly what to do with them.'

Fraser raised his head and looked forlornly at West.

'Sorry,' he said as his eyes glazed over. 'I don't know what else to say but sorry.'

'Sometimes sorry is never enough.'

'So, what will happen to me now?'

'Well,' said Munro, 'I expect your wife will divorce you, your children will disown you, and your dog, if you have one, will probably bite you.'

'And apart from that,' said West, 'you'll be in court tomorrow. Iain Fraser, I am charging you under section 1 of the Criminal Justice Act for the murder of Nancy Wilson. You are not obliged to say anything but anything you do say will be noted and may be used in evidence. Do you understand?'

Chapter 18

Despite an obsession with puzzle books and crosswords, an uncanny knack of slaughtering his opponents when challenged to a game of Mastermind or Connect 4, and a flair for memorising names, numbers, and faces, Duncan's teachers – based on his inability to complete an exam paper or concentrate in class – believed his best prospects on leaving school lay in the shipyards of Govan or the steelworks of Motherwell.

His parents, however, shuddering at the thought of him following in his father's footsteps, encouraged his desire to bring law and order to the streets of Inverclyde and sent him to college in Kincardine where, heeding the advice of Dr Seuss that there was no point trying to fit in if you were born to stand out, Duncan became odds-on favourite as the candidate most likely to be expelled.

After a successful graduation and a probationary period in the shadow of a by-the-book jobsworth, he returned home where, after a couple of years spent arresting the jakeys and neds littering the schemes in his home town, he quickly learned under the fortuitous guidance of one James Munro, that in order to be cool, one had to be calm and collected.

'Alright,' he said as he ambled into the office. 'What's up with you lot? Have you been at the happy pills again?'

'I don't know what you mean,' said West, smiling.

'When I left here, you looked as though you were heading for a family funeral, by which I mean, every single member of your family.'

'I know,' said West, 'but as they say, you never know what's around the corner.'

'Well, if it's any help, McPherson couldn't remember the name but he recognised the photo. He's identified Fraser as the fella in the pub with Nevin.'

'Thanks, mate, but I sent you on a bit of a wild goose chase, I'm afraid. Fraser's admitted it. He's given us the whole story. Dougal's banging out the report for the fiscal as we speak.'

'Smashing,' said Duncan. 'Well, despite the fact that I've been all the way to Dumfries and back, I'll make a brew. Who's for a cup?'

'You're alright,' said Dougal, 'I'm busy.'

'Not for me thanks,' said West. 'I'm fine.'

'Chief?'

'No, no. Thanks all the same,' said Munro, 'too much tea with my tablets makes me want to… let's just say it has an adverse effect on my well-being.'

Duncan leaned against the counter, scratched the stubble on his chin, and stared at his colleagues one by one.

'What's going on here?' he said. 'Are you lot coming down with something? Next thing you'll be telling me you're not hungry.'

'It's a contagious dose of relief, that's all,' said West. 'And the best way to treat it is not with tea but with a half-decent twelve-year-old.'

'Are you doing this on purpose, miss? Teasing me with alcohol when you know I've a drive ahead of me?'

'You've heard of Uber, haven't you?'

'Oh no, no,' said Duncan, 'I'm not jumping a taxi where the driver relies on his sat nav because he can't speak English.'

'That's not very PC, surely you mean *because he can't read a map?*'

'Aye. Of course I do.'

'Don't worry,' said West, 'you're not missing out. We haven't hit the booze just yet.'

Rankled by their uncharacteristically insouciant attitude, Duncan, suspecting he may fall victim to an office prank, stood with his back to the door lest the only available chair collapse beneath him.

'Can someone enlighten me?' he said, keeping a watchful eye on their every move. 'If this Fraser fella's the guilty party, then how could we have been so wrong about Nevin when all the evidence was pointing towards him?'

'You're forgetting,' said West, 'all the evidence was pointing at McPherson too.'

'Aye I know but…'

'You weren't wrong about Nevin,' said Munro, 'you were on the money right enough. He and Fraser were in it together.'

'Would you care to stick some meat on those bones, chief?'

'My pleasure, laddie. It was Nevin who concocted the plan and a relatively simple one it was too. He arrived at the leisure centre on his motorbike as though he were expected and, as we discussed earlier, he spent the whole day going about his business, hidden in plain sight, as it were. Fraser arrives that evening and waits until the CCTV has been disabled; then he pops inside and Nevin gives him the gloves to wear so he doesnae leave his prints all over the place.'

'Okay,' said Duncan, 'I get that but what about McPherson? Why was Nevin framing him? I mean, he didn't go to the centre with the intention of killing Miss Wilson, did he?'

'Quite right,' said Munro. 'He did not. Unfortunately for Nevin, he didnae count on Fraser going ballistic and battering Miss Wilson to death but in his favour, he already had a half-cocked plan to cover his backside should things go awry.'

'Why?'

'Because the only folk who knew about the money were Galbraith, Wilson, and McPherson. If he didnae incriminate McPherson in the theft, then McPherson would know it was them who went after the money.'

'Okay,' said Duncan. 'Now I'm with you. So when they didn't get what they were after, you know, the whereabouts of the safe and the code to open it…'

'That's right,' said West. 'When they didn't get that, Nevin whipped round to Wilson's gaff the following day to look for it, safe in the knowledge that there was no way she was going to walk through the door and catch him at it.'

Duncan, looking as deflated as a punctured lilo, finished his tea and stared blankly at the empty mug.

'Why the long face?' said West. 'You should be happy, we've got a right result! Three for the price of two!'

'Oh aye,' said Duncan, 'I am. Ecstatic.'

'Oh for God's sake, don't sit there moping, spit it out.'

'There's something missing' said Duncan. 'There's one piece of the proverbial jigsaw I just can't figure.'

'See here,' said Dougal smiling, 'we've got them all, pal. All three of them banged up. What more are you wanting?'

'The connection.'

'What connections that? I don't know what you mean.'

Munro, allowing himself the kind of subtle smile normally reserved for smug parents whose offspring had trounced the opposition on school sports day, turned to face the room.

'I do,' he said proudly. 'Your inquisitiveness, Duncan, is commendable. I'm telling you, Charlie, you need to watch this one, he'll go far.'

'Easy on the praise,' said West, 'if his head swells any more, he won't get out the door.'

'So it's a connection you're wanting. And what connection would that be?'

In a rare display of self-doubt Duncan, fearing his lack of experience was about to open him up to ridicule from his colleagues, winced as he proffered the question.

'Galbraith and Wilson,' he said nervously. 'Why would Galbraith give Nancy Wilson a hundred grand?'

Dougal, embarrassed by the fact that he'd missed something so obvious, glanced furtively at West and lowered his head.

'Well, I'm glad to see someone's still concentrating,' said Munro. 'Perhaps young Dougal would like to furnish you with the answer.'

'Me?'

'Aye, laddie. You. Wilson's CV. You've not finished reading it.'

'Jeez-oh! I clean forgot about that!' said Dougal. 'Okey-dokey, where did I get to?'

'Just tell us about her education.'

'Right you are. She got an HNC and an HND from Dumfries and Galloway college, and before that she went to secondary school at St Joseph's. Her primary school was in... Palnackie.'

'Palnackie?' said Duncan. 'Is that not where Galbraith lives?'

'It is indeed,' said Munro. 'It's where he lives and where he works, as the headmaster of the school.'

'This is turning into "book at bedtime",' said West. 'Give me a second and I'll grab a pillow before you carry on.'

'If you're bored, Charlie, I'll happily leave you to figure it out for yourself.'

'No, no, don't do that, chief,' said Duncan. 'Do you know something we don't?'

Munro, hands clasped firmly behind his back, returned to the window and gazed down at the street below.

'The call I took earlier,' he said, 'while Mr McLeod was here. It was from DCI Clark in Dumfries. He was telephoning to convey his thanks for my assistance in the apprehension of Galbraith…'

'Good for you.'

'…and to let me know that he'd already made his debut in court. He's to be prosecuted on behalf of HMRC for falsifying accounts, fraud and anything else they can throw at him. Oh and of course, the council will be wanting their money back too.'

'How's he going to do that?' said West. 'He can't be that minted, can he? Surely he's spent it all?'

'Not all of it,' said Munro. 'You're forgetting that Miss Wilson was holding one hundred thousand pounds which he'd stolen from Flora MacDonald. The rest will come from the sale of his house, his holiday home, and his boat.'

'Boat? Blimey,' said West, 'he didn't hold back, did he? If I'd half-inched all that cash, the last thing I'd do is flash it around.'

'Och, he wasnae that stupid,' said Munro. 'He made a point of letting everybody know that his wealth had been accumulated over a long period of time as a result of some very shrewd investments courtesy of his old pal Jack MacDonald.'

'Where exactly are you going with all this?' said West. 'Because wherever it is, can we get there quick, please? I'm dying of thirst.'

Munro turned to face West and smiled.

'Just for you, Charlie,' he said, 'I shall cut to the chase. Galbraith's not got a mark against his name so, imagine Clark's surprise when Galbraith's DNA found a match on the database.'

'What? How so?' said Dougal. 'If he's not been in trouble before then how could that be?'

'Nancy Wilson,' said Munro, 'is the illegitimate daughter of one Archibald Alpin Galbraith.'

'Well, well, well,' said West, 'this is getting interesting after all. And the mother? Some floozie from out of town, I imagine?'

'Quite the opposite Charlie. It was Flora MacDonald. Duncan, you're awful quiet, have you nothing to say?'

'I'm just thinking, chief. Palnackie, it's not exactly going like a fair, is it? I mean, it's a wee village, right? So I'm guessing if Nancy Wilson was the result of a wotsit between Galbraith and MacDonald, then there's no way they'd have been able to keep it quiet.'

'Quite right,' said Munro. 'They couldnae. When Flora fell pregnant, her husband Jack believed the child was his and Flora wasnae about to correct him on the matter, but more importantly she couldnae run the risk of giving birth either. Jack and Galbraith were as different as they come, she'd have been rumbled in a thrice, so she took herself off to have the bairn while Jack was manning the Post Office, but she returned empty handed.'

'Empty handed?' said West. 'What do you mean?'

'She told Jack the bairn had died at birth.'

'Oh no,' said Duncan, 'that's not right! That's not right at all! The poor man must have been beside himself with grief.'

'How can you be sure about this?' said West.

'Because there's a wee headstone in the kirkyard bearing her name and the inscription "taken at birth".'

'So, what really happened to her?' said West. 'Was she given away?'

'Aye she was,' said Munro. 'She was given up for adoption and raised as Nancy Wilson in Kippford.'

'Where's that?'

'Across the water from Palnackie.'

'And did Galbraith know about this?' said West. 'Did he know that his daughter had been secreted away?'

'He arranged it,' said Munro. 'The man was more interested in protecting his reputation than raising his only child.'

'So that's why he gave her a hundred grand,' said Duncan. 'Guilt.'

'Right enough. I imagine he thought a wee gift to see her through life might ease his conscience.'

'And the wee locket? I'm guessing that belonged to Flora MacDonald, am I right?'

'Well, I cannae say for sure, laddie, but I think it's safe to assume that it probably did, aye.'

Epilogue

For Jean Munro, an overworked nurse married to an aspiring young detective with a mind as sharp as a pin and an almost paternal instinct to protect those around him, the decision not to raise a family, based on ever-changing shifts, a spiralling mortgage, and a husband who spent more time with the dead and the dying than lolling about in her arms, was not a conscious one but a natural development borne of circumstance.

For James Munro, however, the role of doting godparent to the offspring of numerous close friends – a duty fraught with the inherent danger of taking care of their welfare should their natural parents succumb to an untimely demise – was recompense enough for the lack of an heir to his meagre estate.

Cradling a large Balvenie as he relaxed on the sofa, he smiled ruefully to himself and wondered what his late wife would make of the dysfunctional bunch of misfits he'd inadvertently adopted as his own; the headstrong daughter with a Taurean bent for kicking-off like a bull in a china shop, the studious son who preferred the company of a computer and socialising with fish, and the chip off the old block whose laid-back demeanour and cocky smile assured him of success.

* * *

'I've been thinking,' said West as she unpacked the takeaways, 'have you noticed how good things come in threes?'

'Is that so?' said Munro. 'Would you care to elucidate?'

'Three little pigs. Three French hens. Three blind mice...'

'That all sounds well and good if you're of a mind to open a farm, lassie.'

'...and of course, Fraser, McPherson, and Nevin.'

'You surprise me, Charlie.'

'How?'

'I'd have thought top of your list would have been ham, cheese and pickle. Bacon, lettuce and tomato. And pie, mash, and beans.'

'Very funny. So, how are you feeling?'

'Aye okay,' said Munro. 'A wee bit tired perhaps but that's to be expected.'

'No twinges? No palpitations? No shortness of breath?'

'None.'

'Good. Right then, as it's your last night chez West, should we crack open the wine?'

'It would be foolish not to. And what delight did you bring to complement this delightful fish supper?'

'Nothing fancy, just a bog-standard Beaujolais, but it's red, it's wet, and it's alcohol.'

'I can see no problem with that,' said Munro as he eyed her plate. 'Did you not get yourself fish as well?'

'Nope. I got myself a haggis supper with a sausage on the side.'

'Dear God, you'll be dyeing your hair orange and drinking Irn-Bru for breakfast next.'

Munro doused his supper with a generous helping of salt followed by a good-sized dollop of brown sauce and raised his glass.

'Cheers,' he said. 'Your very good health.'

'Yours more than mine.'

'And congratulations on bagging those three villains, it's a job well done.'

'I'm not taking the credit for that,' said West. 'It was a team effort, present company included.'

'Speaking of which, did you notice how one particular member of said team went over and beyond the call of duty?'

'You're talking about Duncan, aren't you?'

'What do you think?'

'I think you're right,' said West. 'He's been a diamond throughout the whole investigation, not to mention yours. I'd even go so far as to say he's given Dougal a right old run for his money.'

'You're not wrong there, Charlie; he's shown his mettle right enough. Dougal is peerless when it comes to solving problems, I'll give him that, but Duncan's the one who finds them. Mark my words, that boy could find a rotten egg in a farm full of battery hens.'

'Not while I'm eating please,' said West. 'Do you know what I like about him most?'

'Remember he's spoken for.'

'He's got a soft side. He's not all chewing gum and bravado.'

'Which is why he's in a relationship with a single mother and dotes on her son as if he were his own.'

West downed her tools, sipped her wine, and stared at Munro.

'I'm going to do it,' she said. 'I've decided. I'm going to recommend he takes his exams.'

'Calm your beans,' said Munro. 'I'd ask him first, Charlie, we may think he's destined for greater things but some folk are happy with their lot. Aside from that, I'm glad. I think it's the right decision.'

'Good. Now I've got a question for you.'

'On you go.'

'Fraser. What was all that about in the interview room, you know, when you were trying to mitigate his behaviour because of stress?'

'Simply that, Charlie. The chap's entitled to know what help there is at his disposal.'

'Yeah, but he flipping-well topped someone, didn't he?'

'See here, Charlie,' said Munro, waving a forkful of haddock in her face, 'let's say you were out for the evening and, forgive me if this reminds you of your old habits, but let's say you were blootered and you took offence at something somebody said, and consequently gave them a wee smack. They call the police, you're arrested, convicted of assault, and handed a custodial. Would you say that was fair?'

'No! Of course not,' said West. 'I didn't know what I was doing.'

'Aye, maybe, but drunk or otherwise, are you still not accountable for your actions?'

'Yes but there were extenuating circumstances.'

'By which you mean you were under the influence?'

'Yeah.'

'Well, the situation's no different for that Fraser fellow. It's possible, not proven, that he reacted the way he did because of abnormally high stress levels. It's not different to being intoxicated. Apart from one thing.'

'And what's that?'

'You became intoxicated through choice and by your own hand. His situation may have arisen because of circumstances beyond his control.'

'You think so?'

'I know so,' said Munro. 'See here, Charlie, I'm not defending the fellow. I'm in the business of finding and convicting those who have broken the law, but I'll not send a man to the gallows for stealing a mince pie just because he was hungry.'

'Okay. Point taken,' said West. 'So, what's happening tomorrow, have you got a plan, Stan?'

'A vague one,' said Munro as drained his glass. 'I've some chores to attend to.'

'Nothing too strenuous, I hope. Remember what McLeod said.'

'Just a wee spot of decorating. Some painting in fact. There's nothing too strenuous about that.'

'No,' said West, 'but you might die of boredom.'

'If you studied mindfulness,' said Munro as he topped up their glasses, 'you'd realise the benefits of such a task. It's very relaxing, therapeutic even.'

'So is a large Balvenie,' said West, 'and I know which one I'd rather choose. Will you be okay to drive back in the morning or do you want me to give you a lift?'

Munro glanced at West with a knowing wink.

'If it wasn't for a fundamental flaw in your generous offer Charlie, I'd gladly accept.'

'What flaw?'

'If you give me a lift, then I shall be without my car.'

'Good point. I know, we'll take yours.'

'And how will you get back?'

'Doesn't quite work, does it?' said West. 'Oh bugger it, you'll be fine. If you get in a fix, just give me a bell.'

'And yourself, lassie?' said Munro. 'What does the new day hold in store for you?'

'Oh there's all that lovely paperwork to look forward to for a start…'

'You cannae make a rainbow without rain, Charlie.'

'…and knowing my luck, as soon as I walk through the door, DCI Elliot will have a festering corpse at the bottom of an abandoned mineshaft that needs looking into, which means, all in all, it should be one hell of a rainbow.'

'And that's why you like the job, Charlie, because there's nothing mundane about it. In fact, it's positively fascinating. Aye, that's the word, fascinating.'

Character List

JAMES MUNRO (RETIRED) – Convalescing from open-heart surgery, Munro, unable to relax in the company of dolphins and eagles, heeds the call of a perplexed colleague in Dumfries and becomes embroiled in the discovery a missing person.

DI CHARLOTTE WEST – With Munro's health a major concern, West welcomes the diversion of a motiveless crime involving the body of a swimming instructor found floating in a leisure pool.

DS DOUGAL McCRAE – Taking the helm during the early stages of the investigation, Dougal finds some plausible suspects but much to his chagrin, each without a motive.

DC DUNCAN REID – Dividing his time between West and the floating cadaver, and surreptitiously aiding Munro in his quest to identify the missing person, Duncan finds himself stretched to breaking point.

DCI GEORGE ELLIOT – The ebullient DCI Elliot steps in to quietly guide West out of a maze of tangled emotions concerning her mentor's health following surgery.

DR ANDY MCLEOD – Forensic pathologist Andy McLeod imparts some disturbing news concerning the body in the pool whilst trying to cajole a harried West on a date.

NANCY WILSON – Employed at the leisure centre, the vegetarian fitness instructor has few friends and fewer enemies which leaves detectives scratching their heads when an apparently motiveless attack leaves her for dead.

ARCHIE GALBRAITH – Unofficial spokesman for a small village community, Galbraith, successful businessman and headmaster at the local school, tries to hide when his cloak of integrity goes up in flames.

RUPERT LEA – A quiet, unassuming loner with an unhealthy interest in the internet and women of a certain age finds himself at the centre of an investigation when the object of his desire is found dead.

JOHN NEVIN – A groundsman of questionable experience with a knack for catching anything that falls off the back of a lorry, Nevin finds himself as the focus of attention when his ex-girlfriend suffers horrific injuries at the hands of an assailant.

CRAIG MCPHERSON – An aspiring boxer who spent more time on the canvas than Vincent van Gogh, McPherson, a jobbing labourer and handyman, will do anything for cash if the price is right.

IAIN FRASER – A talented builder with an eye for perfection, a loving wife and two teenage daughters, Fraser finds a decline in work a strain on his resources and soon seeks other ways of supplementing his income.

If you enjoyed this book, please let others know by leaving a quick review on Amazon. Also, if you spot anything untoward in the paperback, get in touch. We strive for the best quality and appreciate reader feedback.

editor@thebookfolks.com

www.thebookfolks.com

ALSO BY PETE BRASSETT

In this series:

SHE – book 1
AVARICE – book 2
ENMITY – book 3
DUPLICITY – book 4
TERMINUS – book 5
TALION – book 6
PERDITION – book 7
RANCOUR – book 8
TURPITUDE – book 10
HUBRIS – book 11

Other titles:

THE WILDER SIDE OF CHAOS
YELLOW MAN
CLAM CHOWDER AT LAFAYETTE AND SPRING
THE GIRL FROM KILKENNY
BROWN BREAD
PRAYER FOR THE DYING
KISS THE GIRLS

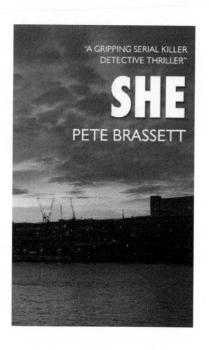

SHE

With a serial killer on their hands, Scottish detective
Munro and rookie sergeant West must act fast to trace a
woman observed at the crime scene. Yet discovering her
true identity, let alone finding her, proves difficult. Soon
they realise the crime is far graver than either of them
could have imagined.

AVARICE

A sleepy Scottish town, a murder in a glen. The local police chief doesn't want a fuss and calls in DI Munro to lead the investigation. But Munro is a stickler for procedure, and his sidekick Charlie West has a nose for a cover up. Someone in the town is guilty, will they find out who?

ENMITY

When it comes to frustrating a criminal investigation, this killer has all the moves. A spate of murders is causing havoc in a remote Scottish town. Enter Detective Inspector Munro to catch the red herrings and uncover an elaborate and wicked ruse.

DUPLICITY

When a foreign worker casually admits to the murder of a local businessman, detectives in a small Scottish town guess that the victim's violent death points to a more complex cause. Money appears to be a motive, but will anyone believe that they might be in fact dealing with a crime of passion?

TERMINUS

Avid fans of Scottish detective James Munro will be worrying it is the end of the line for their favourite sleuth when, battered and bruised following a hit and run, the veteran crime-solver can't pin down a likely suspect.

TALION

A boy finds a man's body on a beach. Police quickly suspect foul play when they discover he was part of a local drugs ring. With no shortage of suspects, they have a job pinning anyone down. But when links to a local business are discovered, it seems the detectives may have stumbled upon a much bigger crime than they could have imagined.

PERDITION

A man is found dead in his car. A goat is killed with a crossbow. What connects these events in a rural Scottish backwater? DI Charlotte West investigates in this gripping murder mystery that ends with a sucker punch of a twist.

RANCOUR

When the body of a girl found on a mountainside tests positive for a date rape drug, police suspect a local Lothario is responsible. He certainly had the means, motive and opportunity. But is this really such a cut and dry case? What are the detectives missing?

TURPITUDE

A murdered jeweller, a series of bungled moped robberies and several fingers found at a refuse site. What connects these events? That's what DI Charlie West and her team must find out, with a little bit of help from Munro. But will the latter be too distracted by his new friend to be of much help?

HUBRIS

When a dead sailor is found in a boat, detective Charlie West is tasked with finding out why. But getting answers from a tight-knit Scottish fishing community won't be easy, and besides, has the killer completely covered their tracks?

For more great books, visit: www.thebookfolks.com

Made in the USA
Middletown, DE
29 October 2020